Escape to the Alaskan Wild

The Journey North
An Alaskan Adventure Novel
By Charles Kalmon
(Book One)

Thank you

There is never-ending gratitude that must be showered upon the deserving. Most importantly, I must thank my mom and my dad. Without them, I would not be. Each in their own way, has given me the tools I need to navigate life with some degree of certainty. For them, I am always grateful.

Jenny Newell deserves much thanks. She illustrated the three books in this series, and did all of the cover work. To say the least, she is talented. Jenny is an art teacher and an artist who has the ability to hear a description from me, and put it on paper in the form of a pencil or charcoal drawing. I find that an incredible talent.

Beyond her artistic talents, Jenny enjoys most everything in the great outdoors. She has hunted and fished across the country. Her endeavors definitely help her to understand animal anatomy, and the animals she draws. Thank you, Jenny.

Chapter 1
Tragedy!

I ran from the noise and confusion of life. Most kids that age who run away, run to the city and live on the cement streets and do stupid things like prostitution and drugs. They, not me! I hated suburban and city life. Suburbia was a place where too many people seemed to be caught up in the meaningless hustle and bustle of life. A race being run with the end result of having nothing more than what they had at the starting line. I watched my parents waste their lives on this thing they called the pursuit of happiness, yet they never seemed to be happy. In reality, it was the pursuit of money that motivated them. I did not want that to be my life. It simply did not seem reasonable for me to do the same thing my parents did. I was young, but I knew what I wanted, and more importantly, knew what I did not want.

Don't get the wrong idea, I was a typical teen in most ways. I had my parents, a "kind of" girlfriend, and a few good buddies. However, hanging out with my friends did not satisfy me in a way that made me want to stay with them for a lifetime. I had an inner yearning for an adventurous life in Alaska. Something very few knew about because I kept it to myself for the most part. From my earliest memory, I read everything I could about the wilds of Alaska. As time went by, I became increasingly aware that there was something more for me than the life I was living. How to go about getting what I wanted remained quite unclear to me. One thing was certain, though, it felt like I was stuck in a meaningless life. I wanted and needed purpose, something that would make me want to get up each morning. So, yes, I felt like a laboratory rat in a cage. That was until tragedy struck and, in a strange way, opened some doors of opportunity for me.

One day after school, I came home to a driveway with two cars parked in it. One was a police car, while the other was a dark blue car with a state license plate on it. There were a few people standing by the vehicles and as I got out of my car, a police officer asked me for my name. After I told him who I was, he instructed me to join him inside the house.

"Sure," I said with some dismay in my voice. "What is going on?"

He was quiet, but once we were in the kitchen, he answered my question. "There has been an accident."

"What kind of accident?" I questioned

"A car accident." And then after a short pause, "I am sorry to inform you that both of your parents have been killed."

I stood silent, blankly staring at him. My breath seemed to evaporate from my lungs like a drop of water on hot desert sand. I did not know what to say. Someone put an arm around my shoulders but I did not look to see who it was.

Finally, I managed, "What do you mean, killed?"

"They were killed in a car accident this afternoon while traveling to a worksite. I am very sorry for your loss."

"Thanks," I mumbled confusedly. No other words came to me.

I stood motionless, my mind picturing a horrific accident. I wondered if the sirens I had heard from my classroom were the ones for my parents' accident. My panicked mind raced wildly. My breathing, forced and labored by this sudden gut punch, made my voice sound distant and lost. Finally, after searching my mind for a calm spot, I managed to ask, "What should I do?"

"Well, do you have family to go stay with?" the officer asked.

"No, I don't have any relatives." Then, after a long pause, "Are you sure the people who were killed are my parents?"

"Yes, son, they were your parents. We made positive identifications at the scene."

Tears streamed down my face. "My parents are gone, dead," I mumbled in a trance-like whisper.

"Well," the officer said, as if he did not hear me, "I hate to sound unsympathetic but because of your age, I cannot leave you alone. This lady can help you sort things out. Her name is Sarah Williams. She has been assigned to your case."

"Case? What does that mean?"

"It means that the state is now responsible for your well-being," Sarah, the person with her arm around my shoulders, interjected.

"What does age have to do with it?" I asked her. "I have taken care of myself for most of my life."

"Well, I can appreciate and understand what you are saying, so let's look at this as a situation that will give us time to figure out what is best for you."

I was confused as to why they were talking about me almost like I was not there, especially since my mind was still whirling with the idea of my parents being deceased. It felt as if they wanted to get this whole ordeal wrapped up and get on with their days. Finally, after a few minutes ticked by with me listening to their conversation, I realized that I did not want to be the focus of attention standing in the kitchen of my house, so I agreed to their plan.

"Okay," I said, with some resignation lingering in my voice. "I will go where you want me to go, but I would really like to be alone for a while after we get there."

While they finished their work, I came to the realization that she was right. It would be good for me to have a place to stay and collect my thoughts. I was in a daze. Things like this are not expected to happen, but they do, and I had to handle the situation as best I could. My hope was that after the smoke cleared and things had settled down, I could make my plans to move away and start a new life in Alaska, the place of my dreams. After all, there was no longer anything here to keep me from moving away.

A few days after the accident, I learned that they were actively seeking foster care because there were no relatives for me to live with. Foster care was not in the picture as far as I was concerned. I did not particularly enjoy life with my parents because they were always gone, always working. I found no good reason why life would be better with some other family. Besides that, I was almost eighteen, and was always the quiet and independent kid who knew how to get things done. So, I got it done. It happened like this.

After the first day living with a host family, and until the state could find a home for me, I was allowed to move back into my parent's house with minimal supervision. After all, I was seventeen when all of this started. It seemed that they were having a hard time finding a family that was interested in a person of my age. I thought that was odd since it would only be for two months. The days came and went, and then about a week or so after my parents' death, a notice came in the mail naming me as the sole beneficiary to my parent's life insurance money, and that money had been deposited in my bank account. Even though the money legally belonged to me, I was still a minor. *Crazy,* I thought, *this has to be a mistake.* As ideas slammed my brain, I made a quick and successful search for my bankcard in my wallet. This was an unexpected opportunity but would add greatly to the success of my plan.

That very same day, because I was concerned that the insurance company and the bank would realize I was a minor, I made withdrawals from the account. In short time I withdrew twenty thousand dollars. The amount still in the bank was, $271,000.00. The dollar amount was impressive, but it didn't really mean much to me other than the fact that the money was going to be used to help me disappear into the Alaskan wilderness. I figured it was best for me to continue to go to school and be good in the eyes of my caretakers. After all, they seemed to forget about the foster care situation and no one ever came and checked up on me. Living at home and being undisturbed allowed me to craft a plan to leave my old life behind.

I had always dreamed of living in Alaska. My earliest memories were of myself looking through picture books in the library and being in awe of the land and its animals. Now the time I spent thinking about Alaska had purpose. I began to do in depth research on remote Alaskan villages. It was really cool because most of these places were on islands or extremely remote inland and coastal locations. It was clear that I could get to my destination, with the toughest task accessing Canada from the United States and then into Alaska from Canada, where I felt I would be free.

My research and ideas became my sole focus, and slowly evolved into what I thought was a solid plan. My vision was that I would travel light until reaching Fairbanks. Once there, I would find a place to live, continue to research life in Alaska, continue to build my pack with all necessities in order to survive at my chosen place in the wild, and to find a way to that area.

One thing became very clear; I had to withdraw more money out of the account. Set up costs and travel costs were adding up to more than I had originally anticipated. Including the first $20,000, I withdrew a total of fifty thousand dollars because I still thought that the bank and the insurance company might become aware of my age and subsequently freeze my bank account. My days were busy, but not busy enough for the sadness over the loss of my parents to creep into my mind. They were good people who got caught up in the hassle of life in the big city. I missed them.

Finally, after tons of preparation, the day to leave arrived. At 3 am I got up and dressed. It was April 1st. I thought, *a fitting day to disappear*. Setting out on April fool's day gave me a sense that I was in charge, and that I had faked being content to live under someone else's supervision. Now the so-called authorities would know for certain that would not happen. In my over-sized school backpack, I packed one complete change of clothes and several extra pairs of socks. I wore the only jacket that I would need for this time of year. The rest of the pack was stuffed with rice, noodles, salt and pepper, four cans of Spam, and a cooking pot with a lid. To save space, the two-quart stainless steel pot was filled with miscellaneous items. On top of that I placed my rain jacket. In the back pocket, usually reserved for pencils and pens, I placed a zip lock bag with a supply of water proof matches and my old man's Zippo lighters, which at the last moment I scraped from his desk. The lighters were keepsakes that my father treasured. His father had given them to him, and I figured they would come in handy out in the wild.

The pack was near full, but one more item had to fit, my 1950 Smith and Wesson .22 revolver. My grandfather had given the pistol to me when I was born. He died months after my birth so I never got to know him. I always enjoyed handling the gun. Its cherry wood handle was worn and shined smooth from years of use. Now it would join me in my journey. With the pistol, I crammed in two fifty round boxes of ammunition. Nothing was left to chance. I had read many stories describing the dangers of traveling alone. There was no possibility for me to accurately calculate what I might encounter on this trip, but I wanted to be as prepared as possible. This made the gun and ammo a wise decision. That was it. Everything was packed. The last thing I did was tie a piece of rope around my sleeping bag and tie it to my backpack. I was ready for my adventure, ready to find Alaska.

Chapter 2
The First Steps

The first step out the door invigorated me. The cool spring air helped to further awaken my senses and liven up my anticipation for the trip. The suburban streets were quiet. I could hear the far-off hum of eighteen-wheelers riding the pavement of the freeway. I had to get to that road, the path to adventure and freedom, and then make my way west all the way to the state of Washington. Once there, I would find my way to Canada and the sparsely populated areas as I traveled north on the Cassiar Highway. The maps showed that this route would take me all the way through British Columbia to Watson Lake, Yukon Territory. This was an extremely remote route, so there would be countless nights sleeping in the wilderness among the bear and moose and wolves. This did not really frighten me in any significant sense, but did heighten my senses and instilled in me a need for caution. In reality it represented what I was searching for. I liked the idea of living in the real dangers of the wild. I trusted my senses and knew that I never wanted to be apart from nature; rather, always wanted to be a part of nature.

I am getting ahead of myself. Yes, the plans were all made, but shifting them into action is another story. The biggest problem, and one I did not fully anticipate, was getting out of my town. I felt like everyone could see me. No one was on the street, but the sensation that people were peering out of their windows from darkened rooms, watching me pass by was somewhat annoying. In one way I felt as if what I was doing was wrong. I knew it was all in my head. As I walked, I brain-stormed ideas on how to make good time on my journey. The thought of buying a bus ticket came to mind, but figured I needed to be eighteen to purchase one. I decided to give it a try anyway. The worst thing that could happen was them telling me no because of my age.

Since my town is considered a suburb, adjacent to a large city, there was a sizable Trailways bus station, and better yet, it was on my planned route. The station was not busy enough to be open all night so when I got there, I read the sign: OPEN at 7am. I looked around and then crossed the street to an all-night diner and ordered an omelet and coffee. No other customers were there, so while waiting for my food, I engaged the old waitress in conversation. She was hard to talk to, but after a while she loosened up and seemed to tolerate my questions. At one point she seemed to gain some interest in me.

She asked, "Where are you going, young man?"

"To Alaska to live in the wild," I replied.

"Oh, that's nice." She said in a charming but disbelieving way. "And what are you going to do out there in that wild land?"

"Live, survive, be me, the person I was born to be."

"Oh, that's nice, dear. Do your parents know this?"

"No, my mom and dad are dead."

"Oh, no. I am sorry to hear that."

"Thanks."

The subjects of our conversation stopped after a couple minutes of this back and forth. As I watched her move around the diner, I realized her eyes were blank and her movements rigid. She seemed intensely unhappy. Maybe it was from years of listening to meaningless stories told by strangers like me that made her unhappy, stories that reminded her of dreams long ago abandoned. Maybe there were too many long nights with no meaningful human contact, a life that was filled with come-and-go strangers, like those who filed in and out of the buses across the street. I found my perception of her interesting. I felt pain for her as she seemed truly unhappy, and I believe she was. There were a few moments during our encounter when she reminded me of my mother.

My breakfast arrived. I gobbled the omelet down in a fashion that would have earned me stern looks from my mother. It was remarkably tasteful, filled to overflowing with bacon and cheese. I smiled to the cook as I paid the bill. He returned a half smile and an exhausted looking so-long hand wave. I wondered if he was married to the waitress. They seemed to share a demeanor that suggested a general lack of interest in life. I walked out of the diner wishing I had not stopped there. I felt sad and alone. It was 6AM, still one hour before the station opened, and because I could not read the bus schedule on the wall, no way of telling when I could get a bus headed northwest. No matter what, I would find a way as soon as possible to get out of this town.

The station opened promptly at seven. I hovered in front of the counter reading posted information, familiarizing myself with the travel routes, and hopefully allowing enough time for the ticket agent to get settled. I figured she would require some sort of identification, and might require me to be eighteen to ride the bus. Because of this, I considered opting out of the ticket buying endeavor, but quickly talked myself into going through with the attempt. With my cheeriest early morning voice, I approached the counter and said, "Hi, do you have a bus that goes to Seattle?"

"Sure!" The young lady behind the glass said, "Do you want to go there?"

"Yes," I timidly said, still retaining my cheerfulness.

"Well then, I need to see your driver's license or state identification card. Is this one way or round trip?"

"One way," I said as I laid my license in the trough under the smudged security glass window.

She picked up my license, ran a quick eye over it, and then entered some information in her computer. She said, "That will be 212.00 dollars," and handed back my license.

I gave her 220 bucks, and with the change was my ticket.

"Thank you," I said.

"Thank you and have a nice trip. Your bus leaves in 20 minutes from door number five."

Dang, I thought, *that was easy*.

As promised, the bus departed twenty minutes later. I was on my way.

Chapter 3
The First Camp

The trip to Seattle was uneventful, and not fun. I was incredibly bored sitting there listening to people who complained about everything in their lives. In the seat behind me, I listened to a middle-aged man explain to the person next to him about how unfair life was. He went on to say that he was going out west to find work because every employer in his hometown refused to hire him. The truth of the matter, I could easily understand through his ranting, was that he was the problem, not the employers. Yet, he went on and on about his unfortunate circumstances. Several times during the trip, I wanted to stand up and yell, "Do something with your pathetic life if it really is pathetic, otherwise, shut up!" *It seems a chronic condition in humans*, I thought, *to complain when there is really no reason to whine.* This is one of the justifications for my departure from life as I knew it; I couldn't handle people who did not know how to live. My parents were prime examples of this. They worried constantly, and I do not remember too many times in my life when they were not complaining about something. That thought of my parents saddened me.

As the bus lurched to a stop in Seattle, I grabbed my pack and anxiously headed for the exit. Outside the air smelled funny, salty. The wind must be from the direction of the ocean, so I headed into the wind. There was no reason for me to go in the bus station; it was highly unlikely that I would travel by bus ever again. After a long walk, I saw the ocean and excitedly trotted to the edge of the surf. What a mess it had been navigating through the city, but I made it. I walked the whole way, somewhere around five miles, I figured. Finding myself at the coast with the beautiful waves gently rolling to the shore made the entire trip worthwhile. As I stood there gazing over the endless expanse of water, I felt the first sense of true freedom wash over my body. It felt awesome.

I glanced at my watch. It was late in the day. After being cooped up in that bus for a day and a half, I was in no mood to sleep indoors. I walked the beach to the north for a mile or two. The shoreline changed from busy roads and high-rise business structures that cluttered the landscape to more rural areas with houses dotting the shoreline. It was not exactly a wild and natural setting, but it was definitely better than what I had come from. I searched for a place to camp, and finally found a place to spend the night. The spot, nestled between two big boulders, was far enough from the water to miss the rising tide. I knew this because a water line on the rocks and sand in front of the site showed where the water visited twice in a twenty-four-hour period. A huge spruce tree had fallen down perpendicular to the rocks and seemed like it would be a nice windbreak in case the wind picked up during the night. All in all, it looked like the perfect place for a camp. I could start and maintain a small campfire because there were no houses close by and no roads that I could see. I worried a little about people walking the beach because I was not eighteen and someone might see me as a suspicious person and report it to the police.

The thought of being discovered and forced to go back home was a dreaded one.

The decision was made. I tossed my pack to the sand and ventured out to gather kindling wood with which to start a fire, and to find bigger pieces of wood that would cook my supper and keep me warm during the night. While collecting firewood, I heard the unmistakable sound of water rushing over rocks. I followed the sound and soon discovered a freshwater spring gurgling up out of a hillside, forming a small creek. The stream of water led toward the beach. I gathered an armload of wood and tramped back to camp for my cooking pot and water bottles. I returned to the spring and tasted the water. It was great. I filled the water bottles and the pan. I would have rice with Spam tonight.

Cooking and eating my supper on the coastline was a treat. I felt a sense of peace come over me. As I finished the last bite of the night's meal, I thought: *How lucky am I to be here in the wild, well somewhat, and on my own eating the best dinner of my life cooked over an open fire and enjoying a night under the stars.* I rolled out my sleeping bag, lay down, and as I would every other night spent in the wild, slept soundly.

Chapter 4
Creating a Path

The gentle sound of the surf woke me. It was a good thing. The fire was out and I was chilled to the point of shivering. I jumped out of my sleeping bag and fanned the fire. Nothing. There was some left-over kindling wood, so I piled that in a mini teepee formation and gently put a match to it. The flames were almost immediate. With piled on bigger chunks, the fire was warm in minutes. I lingered over it for several minutes relishing in the heat it offered.

While warming up, I realized I had leftover rice and Spam from the night before, so breakfast would be as simple as reheating last night's supper. I remember enjoying this aspect of my new life. I did what I wanted to do when I wanted to do it. That had always been my spirit, but at the same time it always felt like what I liked was snuffed out by others. This was especially so with my parents. I could not remember one single word of encouragement from either one of them. Either my actions were ignored, or they were met with annoyance. My parents were so involved in their work and could not see beyond their cell phones and business dealings. In retrospect, I think they were lonely and defeated people.

After breakfast I cleaned my pot and utensils, packed everything up, filled the water bottles, and then moved up the coastline. Almost immediately, I found myself in the midst of what appeared to be the city. I became impatient. I wanted to get into Canada, but came to the realization, after rationalizing my irrational thoughts of a quick trip north, that this journey would not be quick and easy. It was going to take some time and a great deal more planning than I originally thought it would take.

Up the bank I went and onward and into a section of Seattle or one of its suburbs, I did not know for sure exactly where I was in the city. It seemed like I had gone nowhere because the traffic and human activity was identical to the place where I had initially walked onto the beach. This turned out to be a good thing. At a gas station and convenience store, I purchased an Atlas map of the United States. This map book included Canada and Alaska. Outside the store, I found a place to sit and study the book. The first thing I did was look at Alaska, and thus came to the realization that there were very few roads in the state, something I initially had failed to notice. With my finger, I traced east toward the Canadian border and saw that the only reasonable entrance to Alaska was through the Yukon Territory, and inward through Tok. At that moment the trip seemed to be overwhelming. The state of Alaska was so big, and the distance seemed greater than I had originally thought. I wished I had done thorough research before beginning my journey, and wished I had taken notes and brought them along as well.

My heart sank as I considered my options. As I thought about my circumstance, my eyes rested on an advertisement taped to the window of the convenience store that I had just come from.: Float the Alaska Marine Highway from Bellingham Washington, it read. *Bellingham*, I thought, *I saw that on the map*. I turned to the Washington page and found Bellingham straight north of Seattle on Highway 5. Ninety miles.

I did not know for certain what the Marine Highway was but knew that it was a travel route and that I was going to Bellingham. I was rejuvenated. As I walked toward the highway, by luck, I came across a public library. Inside there were many public use computers so I planned to stay the day and fine-tune my travel plans. I now realized that it was unlikely that I would travel up the Cassiar Highway, as the more likely, and less dangerous route would be on the Ferry System. This meant that my original plans took a big turn, and I felt, a turn for the better.

As soon as I got to a computer, I searched the Ferry system. I found out that I could board in Bellingham. I would change ferries twice, and if everything went well, end up in Valdez, Alaska in less than a week. Price did not matter to me, but I found that rather than renting a berth, I could sleep outside on the ship deck; the literature said all I needed was a sleeping bag. The travel brochure went on to say that there were plenty of fold out plastic lawn chairs up there to serve as cots. This sounded too good to be true, but I was excited anyway. Whatever the conditions were, I would accept them. After all, this was my passage to Alaska, my road to freedom. I spent a few more minutes taking notes and then headed out of the building. I had everything I needed except for a ride to Bellingham.

Outside of the library there were several cabs waiting to pick up riders and take them to their destinations. A thought quickly came to mind, *I wonder if I can pay one of the cab drivers to take me to Bellingham.* Technically, I was a city kid but never had a reason to use a cab so I had little idea of how to procure one. There was only one thing to do, ask. I approached the cab closest to me which was the lead cab, and as I did so, I remembered seeing in a movie that these guys line up so that the front cab driver is the one who has been waiting the longest time. His window was down. I approached from the passenger side of the car, leaned in the open window and said,

"Hello, will you take me to Bellingham?"

"Bellingham? That is a long way, over ninety miles."

"Yes, sir, but I have the money to pay you!"

"The cost will be over three hundred dollars, maybe three fifty!"

"That is fine," I stated confidently.

He said, "You must pay upfront, and I need to okay this with my dispatcher."

"Sounds good! When will you have an answer?"

"It will take only a minute or so," the driver said as he picked up the radio hand piece.

The driver and dispatcher engaged in some discussion and then he said,

"Hop in, and lay three hundred bucks in my hand; we will settle on the final amount when we get there."

"Awesome," I exclaimed, as I hopped into the backseat dragging my pack and sleeping bag behind me.

As soon as the door was shut the driver hit the gas and we were speedily on our way. The cab driver was a nice man, albeit a fast and somewhat crazy driver. After we hit open roads we chatted for some time about where we are from and where we are going. He spoke fondly of his family, and how he and his wife and children are very close. I told him about my mother and father, about their deaths, and about how we were not a close-knit family. He said he was sorry for my loss. I said a polite thank you and then we fell silent. I studied the map of Alaska while simultaneously hoping I would be able to board the ferry. Eventually, I fell asleep.

Chapter 5
Bill

When we were about five miles from the ferry terminal, the cab driver reached over the seat and jiggled my backpack which quickly snapped me out of my sleep.

"We are here," he said. "Well, almost. It looks like your total cost for the cab ride is four hundred dollars." I peeled two one hundred-dollar bills from my money roll and handed them to the cabbie.
"No change," I said.
"Thank you very much, young man! I enjoyed our conversation. Be well!" he called from his window as I returned the niceties with a handwave goodbye. With that, he was gone.

With my pack on my back, I turned and surveyed the area. One street looked particularly hopeful as a place that would have restaurants on it. I walked for about ten minutes and found a little mom and pop diner that offered a daily special. The special was a cheeseburger with lettuce, tomato, and onion on it, and came with a side of fries. I hoped it was as good as it looked in the picture. I went inside and sat down at the counter. A polite and cheerful young waitress approached me from the backside of the counter and chirped a sweet, "Hello."
"Hello," I said with a smile as wide as the counter, "Could I get the special, please?"
"You certainly may," she replied, meeting my smile with one of her own.
"Would you like something to drink with your meal?"
"Yes, please, a Cola will be fine."

"Anything else?" she inquired.

"No," I said, "That will do it for now."

"Thank you," the young waitress said, "Your order will be out in about ten minutes."

"Thanks."

She turned and filled a large red glass with ice and Cola and brought it to me, and then went on to serve other customers in the same polite and cheerful way. I liked her.

The burger and fries were awesome; they tasted better than the picture looked. This had always been one of my favorite meals. I dreamed of the day when I would cook my own moose or caribou burgers over an open fire in the wild, or on a wood stove in my cabin in the wild. For some reason a sense of loneliness crept over me as I was gathering my belongings from the stool beside me at the counter. I worried about whether I was doing the right thing, whether finding a place in the wilds of Alaska was realistic. I knew that I wanted that home, but the path leading there seemed incredibly long. My nature was to press on, and that is what I did. I walked out of the diner feeling better because in a few seconds of thought I was able to find my focus and squelch the fears that had temporarily reared up.

Since I had consumed most of my rice and noodles, and all of my Spam, it was time to replenish the food supply. Because of my research back at the library, I knew food was served on all of the ferry ships, but still did not know how I was going to get my ticket, so having a backpack full of chow was important. As I figured it, there were two problems in obtaining a boarding pass: First, there was my age, and, second, I did not possess a Canadian passport. I did not know if a passport was needed, but did know that we would be in Canadian waters at times, and somewhere I had read that a passport was required or suggested. I could not remember which. Again, that sinking sensation flooded over me. *Was this the end of my trip?* The idea of finding a way to access the ship if I could not buy a ticket began to feel overwhelming.

After doing some shopping, I headed back to the terminal to investigate the situation. When I arrived, there was a line of cars and trucks formed in the parking lot, and I could immediately tell that they were people who were waiting to board the ship with their vehicles. The last guy in line was an old man with a rusted out, broken down looking jeep pickup truck. It was faded red and was loaded to the gills with the old man's belongings. The truck was hitched to a crotchety old trailer with what looked like the rest of his life piled in it. On top of that was an old twelve-foot Jon boat turned upside down, serving as a roof for the trailer.

After examining the situation, I cautiously approached him and said, "Hello."
He looked up at me from his fold out camp chair and said, "Well, hello, young man! How are you doing today?"
He seemed spry and happy. My cautiousness waned with his cheerful reply.
"I am quite well," I replied. "Where are you going?"
"I am making my way to Valdez, Alaska, and from there, to my home in the hills."

"Dang, me too, I mean, going to Valdez," I replied, astonished that we had the same destination.

"Do you live in Valdez?"

"No, it is a temporary destination and one step closer to my home."

"Where is your home?" he asked.

"I do not know yet, but I will know when I get there."

The old man looked me up and down with a discerning eye.

"You appear very young to be traveling to the unknown."

"I am traveling from the unknown to the known," I responded.

"I was unhappy with where I was because nothing seemed real to me. People were coming and going with no reason, and that did not seem right to me. I need purpose in my life. This is the only way I know how to find that purpose."

"You sound like me fifty years ago," the old man said as a smile lit his face. "I was searching for truth in my life and I found it. Since then I have lived in a small cabin thirty miles northeast of Fairbanks. That has been my home for the past five decades. My life is everything around there. It is all I need."

"Wow! That is my dream. I think about that every day and every night. Are you a trapper? A hunter? Are the salmon as big as they say?"

The old man sensed my exuberance, and that made his eyes sparkle.

"Yes, to all of your questions, and the life in the wild is incredible. There are many places to live in Alaska. Some are remote and some not so remote. I live on the road system so I have neighbors."

"Road system?"

"Yes, that means I have a road that goes past my cabin."

"Oh, cool. Not a lot of traffic, I bet?"

"No, very little traffic."

"I want to live off the road system. I want to be far away from people, well, for the most part, anyway."

"That sounds like a good plan. By the way, my name is Bill."

"Hey Bill, I am Codi."

"Living in remote Alaska is not easy, but I can help you attain your dream if you want me to. If so, we have a great deal to talk about. After a short pause to do some thinking, Bill asked, "do you have your boarding pass yet?"

"No, I am not sure if I can get one. I am only seventeen, about two months until I turn eighteen."

"Oh boy, they will not allow you to board if you are under eighteen and alone."

"That is what I figured. What do you think I should do? I need to get to Alaska."

"Well, an idea just came to mind, but we will have to be extremely careful if it is going to work. Here is my plan. The ferry does not float for a couple of hours. Come with me and take a look at the spot where you will hide in my trailer. This will get you on the ship and no one will be the wiser."

"Are you suggesting that I sneak aboard the ferry ship?"

"Yes, I am." His eyes sparkled with a delightful mischievousness.

I followed Bill to the back of the trailer where he pulled off the end gate, and then tugged on a huge duffle bag that came out after a minor struggle. "This is where I sleep when I am on the road. It is cheaper than a motel."

"On the road?" I questioned.

"Yes, I am traveling after attending my sister's funeral. She died a couple of weeks back. She lived down here in Washington. Her funeral was yesterday."

"I am sorry to hear about your sister."

"Thanks, she was a sweet gal and I miss her dearly. I wish we had spent more time together."

"Did she ever visit you in Alaska?"

"Yes, yearly. That is until she got cancer five years ago. Her visits were only a couple of weeks each year. We treasured that time together and spent it hunting and fishing. She was my only family."

My heart went out for the old man. I could tell that losing his sister had hit him hard. His shoulders drooped when he talked about her, and the sadness of her loss showed in his eyes. "I don't have any money to speak of, so the trip has been financially difficult. If not for my sister leaving me three thousand dollars, I would not have been able to make this trip. Most of that money was spent on the boarding pass for my journey back home. I figured it was the best choice, when the only other option was driving all the way. This old truck does not have a lot left to give and probably would not have made it through Canada, so here I am."

"Do you have enough money to make it home?" I asked.

"Yes, I think so."

"You think so." I said, somewhat alarmed. "I do not like the sound of that."

"Well, I will make it one way or the other. After all, I have my sleeping quarters with me and a good friend in Alaska who will help me if needed.
Crawl in and check it out."

Because of our conversation, I had forgotten about his trailer set up, so with this reminder, I bent down and peered in. After crawling a couple of feet through a narrow tunnel of Bill's belongings, I found myself in the center of the trailer, directly under the overturned boat. The area was framed with two by four lumber and had a brown tarp draped over it. On the floor was a twin-size mattress that served as a bed. The inside of the trailer reminded me of the secret hideout I built when I was a child. It was in my closet, made out of boxes and blankets. It was my secret place to go where no one could find me. This trailer setup was one of the coolest things I had ever seen. I realized that I really liked this old man. He was different, unique.

"You better climb out of there, young man, otherwise we may draw attention to ourselves and your hiding spot will be found out. That would end a good plan."

"This is totally awesome." I said as I stood up and faced Bill. "Do you think this will work?"

"I believe it will. The ship's crew does not have the time or ambition to check through people's luggage, that is, unless they have reason to believe a person is doing something illegal."

"This is illegal."

"Yes, it is, but for a good purpose."

"Yet it feels like I am stealing from someone."

"Son," the old man said, "it does not cost anymore for this ship to sail with you on it than it does without you on board."

"Well, okay, I guess that makes sense. I will do it."

I changed the subject because my stomach was growling. "Are you hungry?" I asked Bill.

"Very hungry!" he replied.

While Bill replaced the gate on his trailer, I opened my backpack and pulled out two tins of Spam and a couple bakery rolls that I purchased at the grocery store. My hamburger meal at the diner inspired me to buy some rolls for sandwiches. After returning to his fold out chair alongside the truck, Bill unfolded his jackknife and drove the blade through the bread rolls and sawed them open while I untinned the canned meat and sliced it with my pocket knife. In minutes we were eating cold, thickly sliced meat sandwiches; big smiles on our faces but no words on our lips. I knew that each of us was happy to have a new friend.

After we finished enjoying lunch, and as I packed up my belongings, the line of cars began moving. The loading process had begun. Since we were at the very end, we had a little more time. Still, we had to make our move and not let anyone catch us in the act. At Bill's urging I crawled into the cubbyhole that led to the hideout spot in the trailer. I heard him whisper down the tunnel for me to be quiet and that he would pull the duffle bag from its place blocking the tunnel when we were on the ship and all was clear.

It was completely dark and a bit eerie in the trailer. My stomach felt like it was riddled with blubbering butterflies and rambling moths from the moment the old man put the gate back in place. When the old truck rattled forward, the trailer lurched and sent the butterflies and moths into a higher frenzy as they bobbed and weaved in my gut. I giggled at the excitement of what I was doing. *This is really happening,* I thought. *I am going to Alaska! In a trailer! Behind a truck! On a ship!*

Except for the squeaks and moans of the overloaded truck and trailer starting and stopping on its migration to the loading dock, all was quiet. Eventually we rolled close enough to the boarding door of the ferry for the ship's crew to give the old man directions. They told him to drive in and pull to the far right all the way to the front of the cargo compartment. I did not understand Bill's muffled reply, but did feel the bump that was the difference between the height of the dock and the floor of the ship.

Time seemed to move incredibly slowly. There was too much time to think. I felt a twinge of panic flood over me and became somewhat worried about being discovered. *What would they do?* I thought. *Probably send me back home and put me in foster care for a couple months.* That worried me, but, in the end, I remained positive that everything would work out. I remember hearing someone say that if you look guilty, people will think you are guilty. So, when the opportunity came to get out of the trailer, I had to be normal and do what all the other passengers did. After a few minutes of inching forward, I could tell we were deep in the ship's belly. I could hear people talking and as the voices got closer to me, I began to make out their words. Then, I could tell they were standing directly over my hiding spot talking to Bill who sounded like he was still in his truck.

"What you got in the trailer, old man?" One person said as he tapped rigorously on the old boat.

"Nothing but personal belongings."

"Nothing illegal, old man?"

"No, just my junk."

"Yeah, that is what it looks like to me, junk. Why do you carry all of this crap?"

"It is mine, and I like what is mine."

"Yeah, yeah old-timer. Keep moving."

The loading crew was giving Bill a hard time for nothing. *Or,* I thought, *had they seen us checking out the hiding spot and were now playing cat and mouse with us, teasing Bill before tearing the gate off the trailer and exposing the runaway kid, me! No,* I rationalized, *they told him to move on. That was my cue that we were safe for now.*

My heart had been pounding with excitement and anxiousness. For a moment I was in total fear of being discovered.

After what felt like hours, the time came. I could feel the trailer shake as Bill lifted the gate and then started tugging at the duffle bag. Just as this was happening, I heard someone approaching the old man again and say, "You are supposed to be up on deck. After you park, this area is for employees only."

"I know," Bill replied. "I heard the announcement on the ship's intercom, but realized I forgot my clothes bag. I really need a shower, and all my essentials are in this bag."

"Okay, old timer, get your stuff and go upstairs."

"I will. Thank you!"

Bill tugged again on the bag and when it popped out, he bent down and said, "Come on out, Codi."

"Okay, is that guy gone?" I whispered back up the tunnel, as I began to crawl out of my hiding spot.

"Yes, he is." When I poked my head out of the trailer, Bill told me to sit on the bumper of the truck until he had everything put back in place.

"Okay," Bill said quietly, as he came up and around the trailer to where I was waiting. "Are you ready? It is now or never."

"Yes! Let's go for it."

"I will go first," Bill explained. "When I get to the stairs and see that all is clear, I will motion to you. At that time, you stand up and walk normally into the stairwell. From there we should be good to go."

My stomach felt the fluttering butterflies and moths again. Bill walked away from me and opened the door leading to the stairwell.

"Okay," he said in a normal tone while waving me forward.

On his instruction, I stood up and walked to the stairs and immediately started climbing behind Bill.

I am Free, I thought. *This is intense.*

Just as we were taking the final steps up, a ship employee turned into the stairs and raced past us. For a fraction of a second, I thought we were busted, but he cruised on by. Thankfully, he did not acknowledge us, and we certainly did not acknowledge him.

Up top, we found ourselves on the main deck floor, with one deck higher to go. A ladder led to this deck and up there we found a bunch of fold out lawn chairs and some people erecting tents in the middle of a huge open area that would serve as a makeshift campsite. I had read about this and looked forward to sleeping in the wide open while sailing the Inside Passage of Alaska. I remembered reading in the Marine Highway literature pamphlet that for the basic travel fare, a person could sleep up here for free, rather than purchasing a sleeping berth. To top off the experience, just to the front of this area were the bathrooms, which were complete with showers. As I looked around, I figured this to be the Columbia, the ferry ship that would take us to Juneau, Alaska. From there we would make a change to the Kennicott ferry. That meant I would have to climb back into my cubbyhole hideout. After being up top on the ship, the thought of crawling back in there to change ships was not all that appealing.

Chapter 6
Journey to the Interior

The ship changes at Juneau went well. I felt like our plan was flawless. Bill's trailer was the greatest set up for a person to hide in, and because of our stealth and patience, no one ever suspected that I was a stowaway. The Kennicott ferry took us to Whittier, Alaska, where we once again made a successful transfer to the final ship, the Aurora, which took us to Valdez. Finally, I began to feel a sense of ease come over me, a sense of calmness and knowledge that everything would be okay. Meeting Bill where I did was the best stroke of luck a guy could ask for.

Finally, the pressure of being an illegal passenger came to an end. "We made it!" I exclaimed in an exuberant half-yell while standing on the city dock in Valdez. Bill was happy for me. I was happy for me and for Bill. Together we found a way to get ourselves to Alaska. I did have some reservations about not paying the fare to ride on the ship, but I did spend a lot of money on meals for Bill and myself, so I did not worry about it anymore. The thought of not paying was made better when I remembered how rude that first loading crew acted toward Bill.

"Well, Bill, what now?" I asked.
"I suppose we should head up the highway past Fairbanks to my place and then find some people who will help us locate a cabin in the wilderness. If we find a cabin, the next step will be to start on a list

of supplies you will need. Your first year in the wilderness will be the toughest year of your life."

"I like the ideas you have, Bill, and I expected that the first year would be hard." I paused for a moment to think about what Bill was saying. I felt an anxious happiness in the pit of my stomach, and then smiled to myself because I knew everything would be alright.

"Do you know anyone who has an old cabin and is willing to rent it to me?" I anxiously asked.

"Yes, I know a few people with such places, but the properties are pretty far out in the wilderness."

"That is fine with me, Bill, I want to be far removed from the hustle of civilization."

"Okay then, we will drive back to Fairbanks. After we get settled in at home we will talk to some people. Right now, however, I need gas for the truck."

We drove to the only gas station in town and while Bill pumped the gas, I went inside to pay for it. Inside the store, I saw some hooded sweatshirts with Alaskan images on them for sale. I picked out two for Bill and two for me and paid for them along with the gas.

Bill came in counting bills from his beat-up leather wallet.

"I paid the attendant, Bill, we are good to go."

"What? No. The gas bill is mine."

"Sorry, my friend, it has been paid. I owe you so much it is not even funny; it is time for me to do some payback."

"You know that I did not expect this?" Bill said in a hushed and embarrassed tone. "You are young and do not have a lot of money."

36

"Well, fair is fair. You stood to lose a great deal if we got caught sneaking on board those ferries."

"What could they do, kick me off the ship?" he questioned with a broad smile on his face.

"Yes, exactly! That is what I worried about the whole time we were on board. They would not have refunded any of your money either."

"Oh well" Bill said, "We are past that now."

"Yes, we are, thankfully."

"Oh yeah, Bill," as we walked out of the store, "I almost forgot, here are a couple of hooded sweatshirts I bought for you. They say Alaska on them in case you forget where you live," I said with a playful smile on my face as I tossed the folded shirts to him.

"Gosh darn it, Codi, you have to stop buying things for me."

"Yeah, yeah," I said, my smile still in place. Then, "Hey, Bill," as we crossed to the truck and trailer. "Stop at that grocery store so we can get something to eat. There is a huge banner on the side of the store advertising hot deli food. Let's check it out." Bill readily agreed to my suggestion as we got in the truck and crossed the street.

Inside the store we found the hot deli as promised. They had three kinds of piping hot soups, and since it was a cold spring day, I filled a large container with chili while Bill filled his with creamy potato soup. We approached the delicatessen counter and asked the attendant to make two roast beef and Swiss cheese hoagie sandwiches for us. The lady behind the counter smiled and pointed to a refrigerator case that held the sandwiches. Even though there were many different sandwiches to choose from, Bill and I each selected our original choice, it just seemed like the right sandwich for the day. After that, we stopped by the dairy case and picked up two quarts of milk and two quarts of orange juice. With our arms stacked with goodies, we headed to the checkout counter where I paid for everything. Bill was not happy with the speed at which I opened my wallet, but I felt this was something I had to do. My heart went out to the old man as soon as he told me about his sister, and then about how little money he had. Beyond that, he went out of his way to help me and asked for nothing in return. And, on top of that, and it is the best thing of all, Bill had no clue that I had nearly a quarter million dollars in the bank. This proved to me that he was a nice person and helped people out of the goodness of his heart. That meant the world to me.

Outside the store while we were situating our lunch items on the truck seat, Bill suggested we drive up the road for fifteen minutes or so then stop to eat alongside the road at a place called Horsetail Falls. I was game for that.

"You will love this spot. The rushing river and the falls dropping from the mountainside makes it a great place to rest and enjoy our lunches."

"Good idea," I said. "Moments like this is why I moved up here, Bill. I want to feel the wild. I want to find my place, my belonging, my home."

"From what I can see in the short time I have known you, we are two peas in the same pod," Bill replied.

"Yes, we are, Bill, yes we are," I said with a contented smile broadening across my face.

If everyone were like Bill, I thought, *I would have no problem being around people.*

As I thought about this subject more, I realized that to this point in my journey I had not experienced any significant contact with people. Sure, there were the people on the bus and the cab driver, who was an interesting and pleasant person, but he and the others were just people who sold a product that helped me get here. Bill was the real deal. We were well on our way to a great friendship. I trusted him completely.

My thoughts and feelings about Bill were further solidified as we rounded a bend in the road. Instantly I saw two tumbling waterfalls gracefully offering a bounty of water to the raging river below. The sight proved that Bill knew how to appreciate the good things that are offered in the world to those who are willing to see them. After we pulled to a stop, I grabbed the bag with our soups and sandwiches and hopped out and led the way to

a flat rock out cropping beside the falls. It was about fifty feet from the road, and right next to the rushing water. After he caught up with me, I handed Bill his lunch and then popped open my chili. Bill dug into his sandwich; we were both ravenously hungry. We ate for a long time without talking, trying to satisfy the intense hunger in us. Finally, I asked, "How far is it to your house, Bill?"

"Oh, about nine hours pulling this trailer," he replied.

"Is the land you live on similar to this?"

"No, it is mostly wooded with some hills that pass as mountains."

"Are there moose and caribou?"

"I don't see many caribou. They are more prevalent about fifty miles north of me, but there are a great many moose in my area. I shoot one every year, usually right in the backyard."

"Sweet!" I said.

"Hey Bill?"

"Yes, Codi."

"I am worried that I will not get on a piece of land and settled in before winter. I mean, there is so much to do before then, and me being a rookie probably means I have not considered all that needs to be done in a short period of time."

"Yes, that is probably so, but we will find a way to make this work for you. I have a good friend who I am sure will be willing to help you in your quest."

"Okay," I said, in a distant and preoccupied voice.

Something was on my mind. I had to tell Bill about the money I had inherited from my parents, but did not know if this was the right time. Then, as if I unconsciously made the decision, blurted out, "Bill, I have a lot of money. About a quarter of a million dollars to be more accurate."

"Ha-ha, me too!" he said with a dream-like grin on his face. I could tell that he went into a momentary fantasy world. For a little while he was in a place where he had that kind of money. His face told the story.

I left him to his thoughts for a minute or two, and then said, "I have yet to tell you the whole story of my life. My parents were killed in a car accident and I received all of the insurance money from the accident claim. It is in the bank, all mine!"

"Are you serious?" he asked with doubt in his voice.

"Yes!"

"Why did you run away?"

"They wanted to put me in foster care for two months, and I knew that it would not turn out good for me if that happened."

"Why would it not be good for you?" he asked.

Well, besides not wanting to go and live with people I did not know, I figured that in the time with them, I might lose my inspiration to come up here. I felt like I had to get out at that particular time, so I made the decision to take off."

"Oh, I understand," was his response. Then after a few minutes,

"I remember that point in my life."

"Did you run away too?" I asked.

"No, not in the sense that you did. I had a cheating wife. She preferred doing things that were detrimental to our marriage, so I left her and came up here. I never looked back."

"Then it was a good decision, I mean, looking back at it all?"

"Yes," he said quietly. Yes, it was."

"Did you ever miss people from home back then?"

"Only my sister. I had no other siblings."

"Are you happy now, Bill?"

"Yes I am. After all, I just made a new friend."

"I am happy too, Bill, happy to be here and to have you for my friend."

"Yeah," he said. "We are two peas in the same pod, one old pea and one young pea."

We laughed and then sat quietly in thought as we finished our meals, then packed up our trash and chugged up the mountainside and through Keystone Pass toward Bill's cabin. I remember peaking the top of the pass a few miles from the water falls, and then remember waking up as Bill shook my arm.

"We are at my place, Codi!"

"Awesome!" I said as I looked around through sleepy eyes.

Chapter 7
The Plans Get Serious

Bill never once mentioned my money after that conversation unless I brought the subject up. I found that to be a pleasing aspect about him. The first few days at Bill's place were spent doing odds and ends type work that had been neglected during the time spent attending his sister's funeral. Bill had a team of sled dogs, eight to be exact, and had spent many years, as I found out in an evening conversation, running a trap line. The money he made from selling wild furs was the bulk of his income. Because of his age, the work was difficult. It took a very long time to check the traps by dog team in the cold and unrelenting Alaska climate. He considered giving up his trapping, but that meant living without an income.

"Do you still enjoy trapping, Bill?"

"Yes, more than anything, but the winters are hard on me. I am no longer a young and strong man. Caring for the dogs and harnessing them every day takes a great deal of energy from this old body."

"Do you think you will trap this year?"

"No, probably not. It appears that I have already trapped my last season."

"What will you do for money?"

"There is nothing I can do about not having money. What I can do still is be self-sufficient and harvest all of my food from the land."

"That sounds hard to do."

"It is, but I have this cabin, and it is exactly what you are aiming to do. The only thing is you are much younger."

"And far less experienced," I replied.

"Bill, if we are each going to live the subsistence life we will need each other!"

"What do you mean?"

"I mean that you can help me, and I can help you."

"How so?"

"Well, when I turn eighteen, if all goes right, I will gain access to a great deal more money. I can buy you a new snow machine. A snow machine will help you to run your trap line and continue to make your own money."

"That is a handout. I don't take handouts," he said with slight annoyance.

"Actually, it is not a handout," I said. "We can help each other, not just me helping you."

"Tell me more," he replied. "What do you have in mind?"

"Well, here is my idea. You said you would help me find a wilderness cabin where I can live, hunt, and trap. And, as we already talked about a little bit, that means you have to teach me how to trap. That is your end of the bargain."

"Okay. That can work, especially if we get you a place that is close to my trap line."

"That is what I was thinking. You know the land, so that should work in our favor."

"Yes," he said, contemplatively, "and not many people trap anymore, so this may just work out."

"Bill, the big question I have is how do we go about finding someone with land and a cabin?"

"Tomorrow, Codi, we will drive to Fairbanks and talk to a native friend I have there. That will be a good place to start."

"Awesome, and let's look at snow machines too," I blurted excitedly.

"Sounds good. Let's turn in for the day. I am worn out. Good night."

"Good night, Bill."

I laid down on the cot that Bill had set up for me, but could not fall asleep. Snow machines and traps and guns kept running through my mind. I had visions of me in the wilderness checking traps and skinning fur. I tossed to my side with the thought of a huge bull moose falling to the ground after a well-placed shot from my rifle, and then turned to the other side and saw the same scene with a caribou. I must have tired myself out because eventually sleep overcame me and I rested peacefully with the dreams still running in my mind.

Early the next morning I was up and around, fully energized for the day. We didn't even take time for breakfast. Bill sensed my excitement and made short work of his morning chores. We hit the road by seven thirty. On the drive to Fairbanks, we saw several moose, and almost hit a cow and her calf. If not for Bill's zigzag maneuvering of his ancient and rusty truck, we would have severely maimed or killed the two animals. That is not to mention killing ourselves.

"That cow looked bigger than your truck, Bill," I said after he had guided the truck back onto the road and back in the right lane. We both kept a sharp eye out for moose after that.

Once in Fairbanks, Bill began navigating the narrow side streets on the north side of town. We popped in and out of an alley or two, and then Bill pulled into a spot behind a garage that was behind a house that faced the main street in that neighborhood. We jumped out of the truck and were instantly and heartily greeted by a short, dark-skinned man as he stepped out of his garage. He had blood all over his hands. I was mildly alarmed at the sight.

Bill and this man, Alvin, knew each other well. They seemed to be brothers, as each knew what to bring up in conversation to spark the other further in dialogue. After a minute of banter between the two men, we walked into the garage. Bill exclaimed, "What a nice bunch of birds you have!"

"Yes," replied Alvin. "They are all from this morning's catch. Yesterday we caught 20 geese."

"So, it is a good season for waterfowl?"

"Yes, Bill, better than I can ever remember."

"Who is this young bull you have with you?"

"This is Codi. He is a runaway from the lower 48."

"Runaway?" I said with alarm. "I am almost eighteen." Fear struck me. If Alvin thought I was trouble, and he was the man with a cabin, there might not be a deal made with him.

"He looks pretty green, Bill," Alvin said playfully.

"He is, but he is a smart young man. He knows how to get things done."

"Green?" I sarcastically stated, hoping it was not something bad.

"Inexperienced," Bill said, and we all chuckled.

"Whew," I said, as I faked wiping sweat off of my forehead.

To change the subject, I asked Alvin. "What do you do with all of these ducks and geese?"

"We eat them. Some in stew, some salted and dried, and a lot of them smoked."

"How do you catch them?"

"With a 12-gauge shotgun."

"Oh," I questioned, "I thought you said you caught them?"

He laughed, "We natives say caught when we mean shot."

"Oh," I said, "that is cool."

Alvin's use of words was interesting to me. I liked him right away. He was a lot like Bill, and just like Bill, I felt comfortable with him from the beginning.

"There is a paper bag filled with smoked goose in that fridge over in the corner. Go ahead and have some," Alvin invited.

I opened the fridge door and my nostrils were instantly filled with the wonderful scent of smoked meat. I pulled out the bag and unfolded the top.

"Rip a leg off that goose and tell me what a great smoker I am." Alvin said with a deep belly laugh.

After a big bite and a quick chew, I said, "You are a master, Alvin, this stuff is awesome!"

"Eat all you want. It is my pleasure to share with you."

"Thanks, Alvin!"

Bill jumped in and helped Alvin clean the ducks and geese. As soon as I finished a second piece of goose, I helped the two men clean the remaining waterfowl. Bill and Alvin were talking in hushed tones when I looked up and caught the two men exchanging sly looks and interesting smiles. I got the sense that Bill had set up this meeting beforehand. We talked about so many things, all of them extremely interesting, but I thought we might run out of time to talk about a cabin, so as a prompt, I asked Alvin if he did any trapping.

"No," he said. "Those years are gone for me. I was in a car accident a few years ago, and as a result am no longer flexible and have lost a great deal of my strength. Running a trap line is too much for this old man. Why do you ask?"

There was the smile exchange again between the two men.

"Oh, I don't know, just making conversation."

"Okay. Well, for conversation's sake, I have a cabin and trapping territory that butts up to Bill's territory."

"Really!" I said over-excitedly.

"Yes, really. Are you interested in trapping and living out there in the wild? It is very remote."

"Yes, very much so!" I could no longer contain my exuberance.

"Have you ever lived like that before? Did you grow up in the woods?" he asked.

"No and no," I said, "but I read about it my whole life."

"You know," Alvin said, "It is much different in real life."

"Yes, I know. Bill and I have discussed the topic many times. We made a deal that you guys, well him, will watch over me. Will you do that too?"

"Yes, I think we will." My brain felt like it might burst with excitement as I asked. "So, guys, are you telling me that there is a cabin out there for me?"

"Yes," they said in unison. Their plan finally became clear to me. They looked pleased with themselves because they had playfully tortured me, allowing my excitement to build to an extreme level.

"Excellent! Let's go out there now! I am ready!"

"Hold on, Codi, you do not just go to a place in bush Alaska without a plan."

"Yes," said Bill, "We must plan because we want to spend a few days out there to check out the cabin and the surrounding area."

"How will we get to the cabin?" I asked.

"We will take my boat," said Alvin, "and do some goose hunting on the way back."

I was so excited that I could not speak or think clearly. So many things were going through my mind: traps, guns, food, cabin, fur, and all the other adventures that I had dreamed of for so long. *This is finally happening*, I thought, *finally happening.* When I came back to the conscious world, Bill said, "We are done here for now, let's go home and get things ready."

Chapter 8
The Trip Out

The next few days were spent at Bill's place and at Alvin's home preparing for the trip up the river by boat. Under Bill's guidance, I used some of my money to buy tools. I bought a couple different sized axes, a hatchet, two hand saws, a chain saw, two hammers, a couple pair of pliers, an assortment of nails, hinges, and any other item that Bill or Alvin thought that would be needed to make repairs to the cabin and to cut firewood for winter.

The next item on my agenda was to purchase traps. With Bill and Alvin's help, at a local trapper supply warehouse, we picked out an assortment to meet my needs. When the spending was done, we loaded Bill's truck with all the gear. There were one dozen #4 Victor double coil springs, two dozen #2 Victor double long springs, three dozen #1-½ long springs, four dozen #110-Conibear, one dozen #220-Conibear, two dozen #330-Conibear, and an assortment of extra chain, wire, stretcher boards, and some beaver hoops. I also purchased a bag full of lures and scents that would help draw the targeted animals to my sets.

After that we went to the gun store where Bill purchased a 30-06 rifle, a .22 mag rifle, a 12-gauge shotgun, and a .22 Browning Camper semiautomatic pistol. Of course, the guns belonged to me, but because of my age Bill had to do the actual transactions. Along with the guns we picked up ammunition for all, and just before checking out, I decided to buy slings and scopes for the rifles and shotgun, and a holster for the new pistol. I even found a holster for my .22 Smith and Wesson which I brought from my old home. Finally, I felt ready for the trip.

It was already the middle of May, and I hoped to be settled in my cabin by the end of July. That way I could get all the work done before the snow flew in October or November. Also, I would turn eighteen on June 8th. At that point I would check my financial affairs to see if everything was okay. Bill said he was sure I would need a lawyer to sort out the details. I was anxious to get all of my financial business over with, but did not worry about it because I was certain that, in time, all would be fine.

There was one more thing that was nagging at me, so my last stop before leaving on the trip to see the cabin, was at the local snow machine dealer. There we looked at the best machines for the area. After talking to the salesman, the three of us collectively decided that the 600 ACE Ski-doo Skandic WT was the best machine. It had a 154-inch by 20-inch track with 1-½ inch traction paddles. The price for three of them would be about thirty thousand dollars. I made up my mind that I would buy three of them after my eighteenth birthday. One for Bill, one for Alvin, and one for me. Case closed. They did not know of my plan. I think the salesman thought I was crazy after I took him out of ear shot from Bill and Alvin and told him of my plan, but that did not bother me. Bill and Alvin had done so much for me, and they were old enough so that the things they loved doing most were now actual hardships. So, for a small amount of money, I could give them some of their freedom back, which meant that they could again run a trap line. It was totally worth it to me.

Finally, the time came for us to leave. We made our final preparations and then loaded the boat and launched it in the river. We took it slow, as the water was high due to recent torrential rain falls. There were a great deal of logs and other floating debris, some of it submerged, that had washed into the river or been dislodged from sandbars. If we hit a log it could destroy the boat. In heavy river current, that probably meant death for us. After about an hour and a half of careful navigation, Alvin maneuvered the boat off the main river into a small indenture that looked like a pond, but was actually just a sharp cut in and a sharp cut out of the riverbank. I was standing in the front of the boat as we inched toward the shore. I saw small schools of large fish darting to shadowy, protective hideouts in the weedy water.

"What type of fish are those?" I asked Bill who was sitting behind me on a comfortable bench seat.

"Probably pike," he said as he stood up and looked. "Yes, they are pike. Those are good eating fish."

"Wow," I said. "Some of them are huge. Are they easy to catch?" I questioned.

"If they are hungry," Bill said, as the two men burst out in laughter at the joke.

"Ha-ha," I said half under my breath and with an embarrassed smile on my face.

I watched the fish a while longer and decided that I needed to buy fishing equipment before coming back to stay. After a minute, Alvin ran the bow of the boat on shore where a small sandy area jutted out from the shoreline. Bill told me to jump out and catch the rope he had in his hand.

I did as I was told. He threw it to me and said, "Pull it tight and tie it to that log. That will hold us in place." After the boat was tied snuggly to the shoreline, Alvin came to the front of the boat and we helped him out.

"Grab the axes and a hand saw, and we better load the shotgun with those slug rounds just in case there is a bear nearby, or worse, in the cabin." He instructed as we lowered him to the ground.

"In the cabin?" I questioned.

"Yes," Alvin told me, "Old cabins are a favorite place for bears to use as dens."

With that, Bill grabbed the gun and loaded it. I paid close attention because my experience with guns was still quite limited. After the gun was loaded and ready, we headed away from the river, and after a short anticipation filled walk up the overgrown trail, I saw it. There it was, my cabin. Excitement filled my voice.

"My cabin," I said as we all stopped and looked at it. In my eyes, it was a king's castle.

Chapter 9
The First Day

That first day in the wild remains vivid in my memory. Everything was so new to me, so exciting, so beyond my dreams. Because we had many supplies and knew nothing of the cabin's condition, we figured it was best to check the cabin out and determine its worth before carrying all of my equipment to it. After a quick look, we determined the cabin structure was stick built, that meant someone had floated all of the lumber and siding material up the river. Alvin said it was an old trapper's cabin, and that during his times trapping this area, he had used it very little. By the looks of the place, no one had visited there in years. With a quick check of the inside, while we held our breath in anticipation of a bear charging out the door, Bill determined that there were no bears spending leisure time in it. This was a great relief to all of us. There are no shortages of stories told in Alaska about grizzlies that take up quarters in abandoned cabins, and then protect them as their own.

It was plain to see that the cabin needed quite a bit of work, but we knew that with some time and effort, it could be easily fixed. The actual repairs, however, would have to wait until all of my equipment was moved up from the boat. While Bill and Alvin did some more surveying of the cabin, I trekked back to the boat for supplies. On the way back to the river to get the first load, I used my hatchet to chop a wide path and cut the willows close to the ground so we would not trip over the stumps.

The last thing needed was to trip and fall with a load of equipment. After all, being this far from medical help, an injury could be catastrophic.

Back at the river, I grabbed the box of food we needed for our meals. The next load included some pots and pans and one of the boxes of traps. That was a heavy load. After going back several times for the remaining traps, I grabbed my pack and in my free hand carried my Winchester Model 70, 30-06 rifle. On my hip, rested my new Browning .22. Plenty of ammunition was in the last load I carried up to my new home, along with a couple saws, an axe, and a spade shovel. I was happy to have all of my materials carried up to the cabin.

After a thorough examination, and reconsidering our original impression, we determined that the old cabin was in better shape than first thought. The roof was sturdy and there were no signs of leaks. The walls were solid and straight, but it did not have a window and that bothered me. There were two areas on the walls that were framed out for windows, but covered with boards. There were no signs anywhere of window glass in the structure. *Oh well*, I thought, *warm and dry is most important to me in this country. After all, I could buy windows and then bring them up with me next time.* For the cabin to be warm and dry, meant a stove was needed to generate heat. I turned my attention to the old stove where Bill and Alvin were standing, looking it over. It was a heavy-duty Fisher stove. It appeared to be well-made and looked to be in great shape. We were still in the month of May so the nights would be chilly. With that in mind we figured there was no better time to start a fire and test out this old beast.

I went outside and scooped up enough dry twigs and old branches to get a fire started. I found my match supply, over 1000 matches in all, and plucked a small handful from the box and carried them in with the wood. I thought briefly about how important matches would be to my life. Possibly the most important items were my guns, my ammunition, and my matches. Everything else could be found or caught, but without warmth and food, death was a sure thing.

I assembled the dried wood in the firebox, selected a match from my shirt pocket where I had them for temporary storage, and held it to the dry kindling. Soon, the small twigs caught fire and the flames slowly spread in the firebox. A moment after the fire began burning higher, smoke started rolling out the stove door and in seconds filled the cabin. "What the hell," I accused the stove while choking on the smoke. "You are supposed to send the smoke out the chimney, not in my face".

As quickly as this happened, we realized that the pipe must be plugged with debris, and quickly snuffed the fire. The cabin was filled with smoke so we fanned it out as best we could by swinging the cabin door wildly back and forth. It worked and a few minutes later we had clean cabin air and had the pipes apart for inspection. Inside, we found a clogged mess that was, in part, the fault of birds and natural deposits by wind and falling debris. Now we knew for sure that it had been a long time since anyone had inhabited this place. Bill and Alvin exchanged a look that suggested, *what, you didn't check the pipes?* With that, we all enjoyed a good laugh.

After the stove pipes were cleaned and put back together, Bill lit another fire. Slowly, the cabin heated up, and by the end of the day I knew that it would be a great heat source for my little cabin. The cabin door was the next project. It definitely needed some work. My short inspection of the project led me to believe it would take nothing more than a few nails in the right places to get the job done. I retrieved the hammer and nails from one of the boxes that we stored tools in and began the work. Because there was more to the project than anticipated, Bill jumped in to help, and in the process, we ended up pulling the stop jambs off the doorframe and re-adjusting them to fit the door, which had warped enough to let in a healthy dose of winter wind. With that, the door was fixed, and it appeared to shut and lock snuggly into the doorjamb. As we finished cleaning up, my mind extended the thought: *It will keep the wind and snow out, but may not stop a bear from stepping in with little or no effort exerted if he was angry. Oh well, that is what the 30-06 is for.*

The days this far north are long in May; I glanced at my watch and saw that it was 8:30pm. The sun still brightly shined in the blue sky. I giggled to myself as I often did while realizing the beauty of my situation. I added wood to the fire and stepped outside with my compass to check the directions and to see where Bill and Alvin had disappeared. What was beyond my cabin door intrigued me, so after determining north and then south, I took a walk. At the top of the nearest hill I rested and gazed back at the cabin. After only a few short hours of work, the cabin felt like a home. Not just any home, but uniquely, comfortably, my home. That was a great feeling; I chuckled the feeling to memory and visited it often throughout my life. Still in thought, I turned and faced directly opposite of my homestead and saw nothing but trees, open space, brush, and there in the willows, a moose.

"A moose," I whispered to myself. My thoughts quickly switched gears and were now firmly affixed on the moose.

My first instinct was to run and grab the gun, but common sense quickly took the reins. I was always blessed with common sense, and this was a great time to put it into action. The moose would not go far, I reasoned, and if he is here, there are more. Hunting season would not open for a few months. It would take at least that long before I would be ready to harvest my first large meat animal. In reality, I knew that I would not shoot such a massive animal before freeze up. The warm summer weather and early autumn air would spoil the meat before it could be dried or canned. I watched the moose for a while longer and then let it be.

In the other two directions I could see stretches of the river as it wound through the land and could see many small ponds dotting the landscape. They were of interest to me, especially since I had read an article that talked about trapping muskrats above the Arctic Circle. Even though I was not above the Arctic Circle, I figured it was likely that muskrats inhabited those ponds. I had plenty of 110-

Conibear traps for them. Although muskrats intrigued me, my main interest was trapping the beautiful marten, a member of the weasel family. Along with the 110-Conibear traps, I had 4 dozen #1-1/2 long springs that rounded out my trap arsenal for muskrat and marten.

As I looked around from my hilltop vantage point, I noticed great clumps of spruce trees growing along the river and up the hillsides at varying distances. Immediately, from all the reading I had done, knew these would be great locations to trap marten. I was excited. After a short look around, I was ready to turn back toward the cabin. That is when, about five hundred feet in front of me, I noticed Bill and Alvin. They appeared to be engaged in an animated conversation; I saw hand gestures and movements signifying laughter. This made me smile. I let them be to themselves.

I had work to do back at the cabin. After returning there and surveying its interior, I grabbed the only cot in the place, a rustic and weathered looking contraption, and dragged it outside the door to give it a good cleaning. I had hoped it was in good shape, but it was not. After working on it for a few minutes, I determined that it was too far gone and there was no use for the cot in the cabin. I tipped it back against the outside cabin wall and left it there and began to weigh my options for sleeping arrangements. Sleeping bags and pillows were not the issue; instead, it was what to sleep on that puzzled me. The floor in the cabin was made of wood, but it was quite dirty. If we were to sleep on the floor it would need to be swept. I searched for a broom, and there in the corner unseen by me to this point stood an old broom. I grabbed it and began sweeping. My plan was to sleep on the floor until I had time to build a bunk. It would work out fine for now. There was plenty of room for Bill and Alvin to lay their sleeping bags in other places on the cabin floor.

Not only did I sweep the floor but swept the ceiling and walls too. There were spider webs and dust almost everywhere. I opened the door after noticing the dust was building significantly, and with a stiff wind coming in, cleared the cabin in no time. With the sweeping done, I turned to move the small table and chairs back to the darkened corner where they were before I began the cleaning. It did not seem to be the most logical spot for a table and chairs, but I figured someone put them there for a reason, and that was good enough for me. As I moved them about, my eyes fixed on a seam on the floor that ran about four feet out from the back wall of the cabin, and was met by a line that came four feet out from the sidewall. It appeared as if someone had sawed the floorboards in a four-foot square. The lines were barely perceptible since they were filled with years of dust. Anxiously, I dropped to my knees and tried lifting on a board, nothing. I scratched at the line and determined that it was definitely a saw mark I was looking at. I said aloud, "This is a trap door! Maybe a cellar!"

My seventeen-year-old excitement ramped with the anticipation of a hidden treasure. I jumped up and grabbed an axe and wedged it in the crack and twisted the axe head by pushing the handle to the side and slightly downward. The boards moved just a bit. It was true; the floorboards were a trap door. Adrenalin pulsed heavily in my hands as I continued to work at, and finally lift the section of floor. It was too dark for me to get a good look down the hole. I moved the trap door to the side and leaned it against the wall. I then scuttled to the side so that the light from the door could shine across the floor and illuminate the hole to some extent. The first thing that caught my eye was a rifle. *No way*, I thought. *This is unreal.* The beautiful sight of a .30-30 Winchester lay before me. I attentively picked up the rusty, dirty rifle and then after feeling its weight, forcefully worked the action. It resisted my efforts considerably, telling me it needed a good cleaning and a fresh coat of oil. I set it on the table still reeling with excitement. Once again, I bent down and searched the underground treasure chest. To one side I could see two wooden crates. I strained my eyes in an attempt to compensate for the lack of light, but could not make out the writing on them. My attention was diverted by something I saw out of the corner of my eye. After a moment to focus, my eyes recognized a huge bundle of traps hanging on the wall of the mini basement which, I could now see, was about four feet deep, creating a perfect cube. To make things better, it was completely framed with wood. It was a perfect cubby for hiding treasures. I pulled the traps up from the nails they were hanging on and gave them a quick examination. They were in decent shape, but had been there for a great many years. My excitement was now beyond measure. The two crates caught my attention once more, and with a grunt and a bit of a struggle I pulled each up the hole and rested them against the table legs. Still, I could not decipher the writing or what was packaged within. I found my axe lying on the floor behind me, and used the head of it to pry the nailed boxes apart. With a little effort I could see inside the first crate. "A window. A window. Yes!" I was ecstatic. I quickly moved to the other crate and opened it. Inside was another perfect window. I looked up and saw the two framed places on the cabin walls and knew they were specifically made for these windows.

The discovery made me feel extremely lucky. It also reminded me of how unprepared I was for my adventure. I was so thankful for Bill and Alvin. In a reflective moment, I realized that I had been out of place in my old life; that was one of the reasons why

I ran away. The rest of the reason was that I had no clue how to live in my old life. I watched people bulldog their way through life, existing, not living. I wanted no part of that; regardless of my age, I was clearly aware of what my life needed. This was it. Here, I knew life would offer great challenges, and, that luck would likely be very important to my survival, luck like I had just experienced. I knew that for the rest of my life I would face challenges head on and make my own decisions. I would live or die based on those choices. I expected nothing less from myself.

After this short reflection, I moved to a chair and wished that there was better light. Only then did I remember that we had two new lanterns stored in one of the wooden crates that were packed with fragile items. In one fluid motion I sprang to my feet and grabbed the crate and popped the top with the hammer. There they were packed tightly between shirts and pants. As the light quickly faded outside, I hurried through the directions, filled the lanterns and lit one of them. Light. It was a good feeling. It was 11:30 pm. The darkness was gaining the upper hand on lightness. It was dusk in the cabin and especially dark down in the tiny cellar.

With the lantern in hand, I was prepared to explore the last corners of my newfound treasure chest. As I trained the light downward in the hole, I noticed an old toolbox. I hoisted it up from my prone position on the floor, turned to one elbow and looked inside. The contents were strewn about, still I recognized a hammer, an old tin of ten-penny nails, and several other tools for which I did not know their uses but thought that they might come in handy in the future. I turned my attention back to the unexplored dark areas of the hole and lowered the light in a back and forth, searching manner. At the very bottom, I located an old-time square tin gas can with the top cut off horizontally, but with the top piece still attached to the bottom piece by two tiny hinges on one side and a small latch on the opposite side, forming a hinged cover. My expectations were of a pot of gold. However, when I got the can open it revealed an ancient wick lantern and an unopened tin of lantern oil. Since I had no plans to move back to civilization, the lantern and oil were better than gold and would become a welcome addition to my stock of lanterns.

That was everything. My exploration was over. Even though I was tired, my excitement was still running in high gear. I placed my firearms next to my sleeping bag and laid my tired seventeen-year-old body down to sleep. Only then did I think of Bill and Alvin. I jumped up and opened the door. I could not see much, but could hear them approach the cabin. I listened to the two longtime friends living their day to the fullest. Their happiness made me smile.

When my friends entered the cabin, their eyes went straight to the little corner basement and the cache of items from it.

"What have you found, boy?" Alvin asked with excitement in his voice.

I answered, "I was sweeping the floor and noticed a trap door cut out of the cabin floor. I had to explore."

"Good thing you did, I had no idea that there was a storage basement in here." Alvin said as he walked close to the hole and looked down.

"Look at the rifle, a 30-30 lever action, it works." I handed the rifle to Alvin. "Nice!" he exclaimed while looking it over.

"And the traps too?" asked Bill.

"Yes! Tools, lantern, traps, and windows. They were all down there."

"Windows?" Alvin questioned.

"Yes, in those two narrow crates. I could not believe my eyes when I figured out what they were."

"Incredible. Absolutely incredible. Someone was planning to make this place livable," Bill said in awe of the whole scene.

"Well," said Alvin, "it is all yours. Make good use of it."

"Wow, thank you. The first thing I want to do is put in the windows, and then clean and oil that old 30-30."

"That sounds like a good plan," Alvin said.

After that we chatted for a few moments and then Bill and Alvin spread out their sleeping bags and laid down for a well-deserved rest.

I smiled and returned to my sleeping bag and after a long time of running incredibly realistic future scenarios through my head, tired out and fell to sleep.

Chapter 10
Fix Up Time

At first, probably from the intense and beautiful sleep I had, I did not recognize my surroundings in the semi-darkness of the cabin. I could see cracks surrounding the door, reminding me it needed more work before winter. After a few eye rubs, my vision cleared enough to help me finally distinguish my surroundings. With the newly found tools and extra wood from the crates, I would be able to tighten things up. *Too much light,* I thought, *around that door.* I made a mental note that before I returned to stay for the winter, I would have to shop for weather stripping and caulking materials. Their sealing abilities would tighten up the door, keeping out the winter cold and wind while making it snug and warm on the inside.

It was comfortable in my sleeping bag, but that comfort was humorously disturbed by the powerful snores of my two friends. I laughed for a moment at their unconscious symphony and then jumped out of my bag. They did not stir. My first order of business was to boil water for drinking. We had small canteens to hold water, but would need to use the can that held the lantern to store water so I would not have to fetch water every day. As I worked, I made a mental note to buy plastic carboys for water storage on my next trip to Fairbanks. Also, Alvin had suggested that we cut brush from around the cabin and further out in order to create some space to stack wood and work on projects. That was second on the agenda, but not the last task that needed doing, that was for sure. The work list was long. There was a lot that needed doing before winter. It soon became apparent that there was nothing for me to do but get to work.

I pulled on my jeans and went outside to take care of my morning business. After returning to the cabin my eyes rested on the windows. I could no longer resist the temptation of their allure. It was with great delight that I unpacked the windows and held them up to the pre-framed 2x4s already in the walls. They fit perfectly. All that I needed to do was pound the boards off of the wall that were in place serving as covers where the window should be. I grabbed my hammer which was sitting on a chair where I had left it the night before and began banging on the boards. The noise startled my companions, and I heard their grumbling and groaning about the noise I was making, and of the uncomfortableness of the hard and somewhat uneven floor as they slowly worked their way to consciousness. They got up, stretched, scratched, and groaned while admiring my handy-work. It was clear that they enjoyed my work ethic. The two men dressed and then went outside to make coffee. I continued working on the windows. By the time Bill and Alvin closed the door behind them, I had the first window opening board free. I put on my jacket and placed a handful of nails in one pocket and my hammer in the other. Then I picked up the first window and carried it outside to the east side of the cabin where I slid it easily in place. It was a snug fit, but to be sure it would not topple from its perch, I tapped some nails in for reassurance. I repeated this process for the second window, and then collected the boards from the windows cut outs. After measuring them and cutting the boards to the desired lengths, framed the windows from the inside and the outside, I nailed everything in place. The project was complete. The windows were installed; life in the wilderness was looking good.

Hunger pains pulled me off task. I looked at my watch and realized it was near noon. I had not had so much as a drink of water since getting out of bed. I went to the river to get water and realized that this was my first scheduled job for the day, but it had been sideswiped by the window project and other things that popped up one after the other. I looked around and giggled with happiness when I saw Bill and Alvin sitting on a log jam a hundred yards downstream. They looked happy. Just like the day before, I did not disturb them. Instead, I turned and carried the water up the hill to my camp, my home.

Unbeknownst to me, Bill and Alvin had made a huge fire pit while I was doing my work around the cabin. *Shoot*, I thought. *I must have walked by them several times*. The fire they built was still smoldering and after adding dried tinder to the coals of the fire they had made earlier to brew their coffee, I went back to the river to get some flat rocks. After returning with the rocks, I placed them in a circular setting inside the pit and set a pan of water there to boil. I piled on more wood and soon had a blazing fire. My little addition of flat rocks made a perfect spot for cooking with a pan or with a pot. After the water came to a boil, I added oatmeal and stirred it in and removed the pot from the fire. I let it sit for about fifteen minutes and then added raisins and brown sugar to sweeten it up.

It occurred to me as I sat down to eat, that we had completely forgotten about supper last night, so this oatmeal with brown sugar and raisins was my first food in my new home. My taste buds exploded. Even though I had eaten hundreds of bowls of oatmeal, this bowl was the best ever. As I scooped in the mouthfuls, I realized how free I really was. Only two people knew where I lived, and that made me very happy.

Feeling much better with food in my stomach, I made a couple of spam sandwiches for the guys, grabbed the 30-06, strapped my pistol to my hip, and commenced to walk down to the river. I surveyed the area for a second or two and then began walking downstream to have a chat with Bill and Alvin before setting out on my first extended exploration of the area. A few things caught my attention on the boat ride up here, and I wanted to see them up close. The first thing that piqued my interest was the large pile of driftwood that Bill and Alvin were sitting on, casually passing the time of day. After a close inspection, I realized this was my firewood, and I would have to work religiously to stockpile enough wood to heat my cabin through the winter. Winter starts early this close to the Arctic Circle, so the time to start was soon.

As I approached my two friends, I could see that they were smiling broadly. When I got closer, Bill asked, "What did you get done up there?

"I got both windows in and cooked my first meal in the wilds of Alaska."

"Oh, I almost forgot, I made these sandwiches for you guys."

"Thank you!" each man replied.

My pride was apparent to both men.

"You accomplished a great deal of work, and did not need our help," Alvin said more as a statement than a question.

"No, there was no need for your help. It was easy work," I said. "All common sense to me."

"That is what we were thinking, so we came down here and passed the morning like two old men should do."

"Sweet." Then after a short silence, "By the way, I forgot to tell you last night, I saw a moose!"

"We saw it too," the men chimed.

"That is likely your winter meat. Did it tempt you to shoot?" asked Bill.

"Yes, I thought hard about shooting, but common sense took over and I left the gun where it belonged."

"Well, good thing you didn't kill that animal. It would have resulted in wasted meat," said Bill.

"Yes, that is for sure. Wasting anything is something I will guard against."

"That is a great outlook to have," Bill said. "It will serve you well."

"Okay, guys, if you don't mind, I am going to explore the area."

"Perhaps we should save the exploring for our return trip," Alvin said, "Remember, we will head back to Fairbanks tomorrow to finish preparations for your life out here."

"Okay," I reluctantly said, "sounds good, see you later."

"Later," the two men said in unison as I turned and walked back to the cabin.

Back at the cabin I finished most of the cleaning and then went back to the river for a bucket of water to wipe down the walls and windows. I also cleaned the chairs, and scrubbed the small table. After this was done, the place looked good. I started supper so when the guys returned we would share a meal and then hit the hay for the night.

Finally, and happily, Bill and Alvin returned to the cabin.

"Something smells good," said Bill.

"Sure does," chimed Alvin.

"Nothing special gentlemen, a couple pans of sliced and fried Spam, a pot of rice, and some baked beans."

"And coffee too, it appears," Bill said with a smile.

"Yes, I figured you two would want a cup with your meal."

"Thanks," said Alvin, "That is very thoughtful of you."

We gathered around the stove and took turns filling our plates, and then sat down at the table and ate our suppers in relative quiet. I could tell from their silence that both men were reliving their youth. Somehow, I thought, after spending the entire day outside in their element that they wished they were in my shoes. There was a sharp spark in each man's eyes. The day, out there on the river, had changed these two old men, reinvigorated them. Clearly these two old trappers loved the wilderness and me. It became clear that I also returned that love to them, something new in my life: To feel loved, and to love someone in return. It was an awesome time to be me.

It is at this time that I began to realize that I really did not dislike people but did dislike many of the things people did. With Bill and Alvin's help, I was learning that everything comes in its own time. Back in the old world, which seemed so far away, people rushed and scurried, pushed and shoved, and then sat and worried about tomorrow. That, I disliked. Out here we did what came natural to us. We ate when hungry, we worked when we needed to, and we helped when help was needed. Bill and Alvin needed my help. I had more money than was wanted, and because of that, I could give years of trapping and travel to Bill and Alvin. It would start with the snow machines. This was the least I could do for my two best friends.

We finished our suppers, and I do not remember who broke the silence by suggesting we clean up the dishes, but with content minds and full bellies we made quick work of the cabin chores and got ready to turn in for the night.

Good night, Codi." Bill said.

"Good night, Bill. Good night, Alvin."

There was quiet in the cabin, except for the symphonic snores of my two dear friends. Those snores came quickly and loudly.

Chapter 11
Back to Fairbanks

We were up early the next morning and soon had everything packed and loaded in the boat for our trip. The boat ride back to Fairbanks was uneventful. Even though there were wonderful sights to see, the only thing on my mind was my birthday, which was close, and getting rid of all of my financial responsibilities with the outside world. After discussing these issues with Bill and Alvin, we decided that I should make a call to a lawyer in my hometown and have him handle the proceedings. It was the same lawyer who handled the insurance money from my parents after their death. Not only did we have to discuss money, I also needed to make sure that I was not in any trouble for running away. Bill assured me that there was little they could do.

After we contacted the lawyer, he told me that I had done nothing illegal, but since I had run away I had worried teachers and friends. After hearing this, I did feel guilty; in retrospect, I had only considered my feelings, and as I was learning, this was quite the inconsiderate act.

Eventually, this lawyer told me, we would have to go to a lawyer's office in Fairbanks to sign papers and agreements. He went on to say that he would set this up and inform us when to go see that lawyer. This made it easy for me because I was not interested in, and did not understand the legal lingo that was sure to be tossed around. My lawyer told me that, in time, there would be a lot more money awarded to me. Apparently, my parents had more money than I had realized. It would take time, but because of modern technology there was no foreseen reason for me to go back home to settle my parent's estate. The two lawyers would handle it all. On my birthday an additional quarter million dollars would be awarded to me. The lawyers estimated that, when all the sales were finalized, my bank account would exceed one half million dollars.

That is a lot of money. Most people might think that a young person would go and spend that money in a few days, and I could have easily done that, but then I would be doing what I already declared as something I despised. The money would only be used for needs, not wants. The list of needs grew during the days we had spent at the cabin. Again, I realized how unprepared I was for the reality of life in such a remote place, and that meant I would spend money on many essential items before returning to my cabin. Until now it seemed more like a fantasy life; however, because of the time I had already spent out at the cabin, I knew it would be more demanding than fantasy. Reality was sure to make an appearance in my adventurous life, just when is what I did not know.

Bill and Alvin gave me advice about canning food as a great way to preserve it for year-long use. They explained that I could can all meats, fish, vegetables, and fruits. This excited me. As I did more research I created a list of items that would help me preserve food. With my list in hand, I began another shopping spree for essential items. I needed a pressure canner. I bought two. I needed jars, both quart and pint. I bought ten dozen of each. I bought bulk spices like salt, pepper, garlic, and an assortment of "live off the land" canning recipe books. All of these essentials I packed in tubs and began stacking up on a wooden pallet that we would load in Alvin's boat for the trip up river. Thankfully, he had a big boat because my new snow machine would have to fit in there too. As we shopped and considered items, Bill reminded me of a few more things that I would need. One of those items was what is called a turkey cooker. Essentially, a turkey cooker is a propane fueled burner on a metal stand that is used for all sorts of outdoor cooking. It would work beautifully for canning food in the pressure canner because I could easily regulate the flame to control the temperature in the canner. I bought two of them and along with that, I bought four, 20-pound propane canisters to fuel the cookers. I was nearing the end of my shopping spree.

My memory does not allow me to recall everything that I bought that first year, but I do remember not wanting for a thing. While waiting for my birthday, I continued to read, and immersed myself in research focused on the Alaskan wilderness. I bought books on trapping and skinning animals, and books on cutting up big game and cleaning fish. It was a fun and interesting time. I think I learned more in those few weeks than I did in the previous two years. Finally, it seemed, that things I yearned for most of my life, were right in front of me. That felt good.

I woke up the next morning at Bill's, a quiet, small place about a half hour from town. I lay there thinking and clearing the cobwebs created by a sound sleep, and soon realized that I was eighteen. I glanced at the clock. It read seven thirty. I jumped up and went to find Bill. He had coffee percolating and breakfast cooking.

"I knew you would want to get going early. This is a big day for you," Bill said. "By the way, happy birthday."

"Thanks, Bill."

Bill loaded up our plates and we ate a quick breakfast. We did not talk much, basically because of my focus on getting into town. With the taste of breakfast still hot on my lips we were on our way to Fairbanks, bouncing along in Bill's ancient and rattling pickup. Our first stop was at the lawyer's office where we received good news. He told us that there were no problems with money, but had one issue with the selling of my parents' property. My hometown lawyer suggested that I give him power of attorney so that he could sell my house and properties. After I signed the agreement, he could go forward with all transactions. Bill would act as an overseer of events, and would be required to sign off on all transactions. My lawyer was paid for his work and all future costs would be taken care of by him, with Bill's approval of course.

It appeared that the bulk of all my financial loose ends were now settled. When my properties sold did not matter much to me in a money sense, but it did matter in the sense that I would no longer have an attachment to that part of the world. So, the sooner they sold, the better. After everything was taken care of, Bill and I jumped in the truck.

"Head over to the Ski Doo dealership?" I questioned with a playful grin on my face.

"Sure thing, that new snow machine has been on your mind, am I right?"

"Oh yes, and much more."

Bill did not know this, but I had three brand new in-stock machines ready to go. I had given the dealership enough money to entice the owner to ready the machines without full payment. Besides that, they were the prior year's model, so the price was good, and the dealer was happy to see them go.

Alvin was supposed to meet us at the dealership but was nowhere to be seen. Just as I was going to suggest that Bill give him a call, Alvin, in his old Chevy truck, pulled up dangerously close to the glass windows facing the parking lot. He slowly got out of the truck and limped to the front door.

"Good day, Gents."

"Hello Alvin," said Bill.

"Hello Alvin, how are you feeling?" I inquired.

"Oh, fair to middling. The body aches more some days than it does on others. Today is a pain day, not so bad as to make me grumpy, though."

"Good." I replied.

We went inside, and after standing on the sales floor talking for a few minutes a salesman approached and asked if I was ready for my machines.

"Machines?" Alvin stated with surprise. "You can only ride one at a time, young man."

"So true, so true. I bought two extra machines in case one breaks," I said in a playful tone and with a huge grin on my face. "Well, breaks, or I want to give one to each of you guys."

"What?" each man said in harmony.

"Yes, I bought each of you a new machine because you have been so helpful and nice to me. Not once did you ask me for money, and I appreciate that. You just helped out a young guy who was asking a lot from people he barely knew."

Bill said, "That is just who we are. We help people who need help, when they need help. From the first day we met, I saw a young me in you, and knew I would help you in any way I could."

"Bill called me," Alvin interjected, "and told me about you; we set up the cabin deal long before you knew about it."

"Wow, thanks guys!"

"See," I said, "it is things like this that make me do these things for you."

"I do not know how I can ever repay you," said Bill.

"Me either," stated Alvin.

"There is no repayment; these are gifts. I hope you will accept them. I see the machines as tools for you both to continue to run your trap lines and to hunt. This gives me great pleasure."

"Well, thank you!" said Alvin. "I don't know what else to say."

"Yes, thank you, Codi. I am buying lunch, are you guys hungry?" asked Bill as he headed for the door.

"Yes, I am, but first we need to have Bill's machine loaded on his truck, and yours, Alvin, delivered to your house. The dealer agreed to load mine on your boat when we are ready down by the landing."

"Wow, you have this all figured out," said Bill from where he stood in the doorway.

"Yes, it really is a piece of cake. I will pay the final bill and we can go get something to eat."

The salesman and I talked for a minute while Bill and Alvin headed to the truck to assist the shop man in loading Bill's machine. I planned with him to have his delivery driver take Alvin's to his place. Mine would be set-aside on a pallet until I was ready for it. After settling my bill with the dealer, I met Bill and Alvin outside and we went for lunch.

Chapter 12
Leaving Civilization

Time was flying by. Because of some legal situations that arose, I ended up taking a flight back to where I grew up and where all my properties were. All in all, I had to spend just under two months down there. At the end of that time, every one of my properties were sold, and everything that was made on the sales was now tucked away in my bank account. Other than that pile of money, I had no ties to the outside world. I was ready to further my journey that had been on my mind for years. Finally, the day came for me to return to Alaska. It felt good that I could now do it legally and without worries of being captured. The trip to the airport seemed to take forever. Finally, however, I was boarded on the plane, and soon afterword flying north to Alaska.

Bill and Alvin met me at the airport. We exchanged hugs and greetings as we walked to baggage claims. Little did they know, but I brought gifts with me. Each of my two friends received a cooler full of cheese and sausage and other goodies that are prize-winning products from back home. This included some great sourdough bread made by One Love Bakery. From all of my reading I knew that Alaska and sourdough went hand in hand. The guys were super excited to see that I bought them gifts and even more delighted after we got to Alvin's place. There, both men cut through the tape securing the cooler covers and eagerly examined the contents. It reminded me of Christmas morning when I was a kid. The men's enthusiasm and their search for the unknown were great to see. I sat back and silently giggled as each man un-pocketed his jack knife and cut off hunks of cheese and sausage and wrapped those chunks in thick, rough cut slices of bread. What a joy to share with my two old friends.

After all the fun subsided, it was time to get serious about me getting reacquainted with my camp. It was now August and the days were rapidly relinquishing daylight to remind us that fall and winter were coming on fast. We decided to load all the essential equipment in the boat; this meant leaving the snow machine behind until after freeze up. This change in plans made sense; after all, priorities are priorities for a reason. Now that the plans had changed, it was decided that Bill and Alvin would pull my snow machine out to my camp on a sled when there was enough snow and ice. And, most importantly, the guys could give me riding lessons at that time; I had to remember that I was a rookie.

All of the days leading up to my return to the cabin were spent buying last minute items that were desperately needed. I bought some metal tubs with tight fitting lids; they were needed to store oatmeal, flour, and cornmeal, and would keep critters out of my food supply. Plus, they would stack neatly in any corner of the cabin. I also bought a one-year supply of tinned meat like canned chicken, tuna, and beef stews. Of course, my goal was to live off the land, but as Bill and Alvin taught me, there would be a considerable learning curve. I took all of their advice to heart because they had lived in this country their entire lives and knew everything about survival. Both

Alvin and Bill reminded me of the old trapper who gave advice to the young logger in a story I had once read. *To Build a Fire* by Jack London is that story. In it, a young man does not take advice seriously as it was given by the old trapper. The young man freezes to death. Remembering this story heightened my awareness in respect to the seriousness of life in the place where I had chosen to live.

We made trip after trip from Bill's place to Fairbanks and to Alvin's place, and then, finally, the day arrived. The day to head out to my cabin home had dawned. I was excited and probably quite anxious too. After all, I was eighteen years old and it would be three or four months before I would see my friends again. Sure, I expected to see an occasional hunter or a person fishing here or there, but for the most part, I would be on my own. This made me happy. This is what I wanted.

On the day we departed, Alvin had a couple of his nephews join us. He asked them to help load the boat and ride out to assist the unloading and carrying of items up to the cabin. They did not plan to stay the night, so it was imperative that we got an early start. We were in the boat and motoring the heavily loaded craft slowly upstream by seven that morning. If all went well we would be to the cabin by nine. Traveling took extra time with the big load. Once we arrived at my cabin, we made one trek up the hill to check things out. The exterior of the cabin was as we had left it. I cautiously opened the door and checked the interior; all looked good. We immediately headed back to the boat and started transporting my stockpile of goods up the hill. Since it looked like rain on the way, everything that could not get wet was placed in the cabin. All other goods were stacked outside the front door. Before long we had the job done. Because of the weather and the amount of work that had to be done, the four men decided to stay the night. Alvin's nephews would sleep in the boat under its canvas top. Bill and Alvin would sleep in the cabin. A rainy and windy night passed and gave way to a bright, sunny morning.

We spent many hours of the day cutting firewood. During this time Bill gave me lessons in handling the chainsaw. Before I realized it, the day was closing out and it was time for my friends to leave. As we began saying our goodbyes, a sense of loneliness hit me. I questioned whether I was making the right decision; I pushed those feelings back. I had to try this on my own.

Bill gave me some last-minute advice, some of which was, "Remember, there are bears out here, so keep that rifle with you at all times. Remember to target practice once in a while. You have plenty of ammunition."

"I will, Bill. Thank you, my friend."

"Goodbye for now." With that, Bill walked quietly back to the boat with his head down. I knew he did not want to leave. I felt the same way; in many ways he was my father.

"Goodbye, young man. Be safe and enjoy."

"So long, Alvin, see you guys soon."

"So long, Codi!" chimed Alvin's nephews. And with that they were gone.

Chapter 13
On My Own

Wow, I thought, *this is it. This is what it has all come down to.* The thought lingered in my mind as I looked around at the huge expanse of land that surrounded me. After a few more minutes of introspective thought, I trotted back to the cabin and went to work organizing my gear. To make the most economical use of my small space, everything had to have a logical place. I set one of the Coleman stoves on the table, opened it up and filled the tank, and did a test light. It worked perfectly. The weather made it a little damp outside as rain had again begun to fall. Still, I decided to cook my meals on the little stove since it was too warm to light a fire in the wood stove. When the weather cooled, I would use the wood stove for most of my cooking needs.

After I had put some more of my belongings away, I looked around the cabin and thought that I needed more room. I wanted to build a bed out of some lumber I had brought up, but realized that it would take up a lot of room in the cabin. After pondering this dilemma for a short while, I figured that if I built the bed with two-foot-tall legs it would give me considerable space underneath for a much-needed storage area. I dropped everything and built my bed. It was the perfect solution.

Under the bed I stored all items that were not needed for everyday use. I hung my guns on nails that I had pounded in the wall at the foot end of the bed. I was so happy that I had decided to buy slings for the rifles and shotgun, and holsters for the handguns. After the bed was completed, the rest of the lumber was used to build a couple of shelves above the table. After that work was finished, I placed my spices and other kitchen essentials there. And, once again, drove nails in the wall under the shelves for spoons and spatulas to hang ready for use. My cabin was looking like a home.

Hunger hit me like a bat slamming a baseball. I looked at my watch; it was six in the evening. I searched out a can of beef stew, and with shaking hands opened it, and tossed it in a pan and lit the Coleman stove. Within minutes the stew was piping hot. I went outside and sat in the light drizzle to eat my supper. After a few spoonsful I did not have the shakes any more. I made a mental not to let myself get that hungry again. I surveyed the land around me as I dipped hunks of bread in my stew and gobbled them down. I was happy, with only a tiny twinge of loneliness included.

After supper I unrolled my mattress and placed it on my newly built bunk. It fit perfectly. I knew its dimensions before I started the bunk so this was no surprise. I quickly made the bed and then did some final rearranging of goods so I had room to get all other needed items inside. I remembered that there was a great deal of work to do outside, so with a pocket full of spike nails and a hammer in hand, I went outside and pounded a neat row of nails into the exterior walls of the cabin. The row of nails was about four feet up from the ground and would serve as hangers for my traps. I then began sorting and hanging all of my traps. While I was in the trapping frame of mind, I gathered all of my trapping gear and packed it into giant tubs with lids; these I would store outside under the eaves of the cabin where nothing would bother them. After this project was completed and the rest of my supplies were put away, I felt that enough work had been done in and around the cabin and went inside to get ready for bed.

The next few days were uneventful, as I worked long hours on my firewood supply. As I stated, before departing, Bill and Alvin had accompanied me to the log piles on the beach and taught me how to use the chainsaw. I enjoyed their demonstrations because while showing me the rights and wrongs of cutting wood, they cut a great deal of firewood. To further their work along, I would slyly ask questions about this or that, which, in turn, by answering my question with a demonstration, would have the two old men cutting further into the pile of logs. I must have gotten too cocky with my questions as they both took seats on a log. Then Bill said, "Your turn!"

Now the keen and foxy grins were on their faces.

"Pick up the saw and cut, Codi. We will tell you if you are doing something dangerous."

I fired up the saw and mimicked their good teaching. By the end of the lesson, we had a tremendous pile of wood cut. All this wood had to be carried to the cabin and then split. Even though Alvin's nephews had helped me carry a lot of it to the cabin before they left, this is what primarily consumed my time. At the end of day four, I had an impressive pile of wood cut, hauled, and chopped. The rest would be done after snowfall when I could throw eight-foot logs on my sled and pull them to the cabin with my snow machine where I would cut and chop them as needed. In the meantime, I would carry daily loads of smaller branches and other dried tinder for daytime fires so as not to deplete my winter supply.

That was it; my work list was temporarily put on hold. It was time for me to go out and scout the land around the cabin in order to get to know my surroundings better, and to layout the ground work for my trap line. That is just what I did.

Chapter 14
Things Get Real

I awoke very early the next morning, the day of my first excursion beyond the general area of my cabin. I had no real plans other than to walk and take notes on everything of interest. I packed a lunch, ate breakfast, strapped on my .22 Smith and Wesson handgun, and grabbed the 30-06 rifle. As I approached the river, I decided to go downstream for a mile or two, but soon found beaver activity along the shoreline and stopped to investigate. In my mind I visualized sets that I would make when the weather got cold and the fur primed up, which in turn, would bring the best price at market. There was no sense in setting traps too early in the year. After a few minutes of checking out this trapping area, I headed further downstream until I came across a moose skull and rack. It was obvious that it had been cut from the body with a saw, so I knew hunters did come to this area. However, it seemed like they only river hunted from their boats because my cabin and the surrounding area showed no sign of use. This was a prize find for me, so I grabbed the antlers and carried them back to the cabin, and then continued my exploration of the area. This time I went along the river upstream, but stayed about thirty yards away from the shore. The brush was thinner and the spruce did not grow in this particular area, but there were blueberries, lots of them. It immediately crossed my mind that I would have to preserve as many as possible. For now, however, since I was not prepared to pick them, I made a mental note to pick berries when I returned in the next day or two.

Seeing the berries in all their abundance sent my mind reeling with thought. The thought that this *life is awesome* kept running through my mind. I was completely content with my first days here in my new homeland.

After eating a few handfuls of berries and enjoying their sweetness, I began walking, still shadowing the riverbank. I walked for a long way all the while taking in the sights and sounds of my surroundings. It was early evening when I decided to head back to the cabin. There was a chill in the air, and the thought of a fire in the stove quickened my step. Ahead of me, just as I turned down river, I saw movement, nothing big like a bear or moose, but definitely something was rustling around in the willows. I slowed my pace, and as I honed in visually, saw pieces of white that seemed to move independently, but had no real shape for me to identify what it was that I was seeing. Cautiously I moved forward. One hand was on my revolver, the other hand held the 30-06. After prowling forward for a few more yards, I stopped and crouched down, still confused as to what I was looking at. My anxiousness grew somewhat because I still could not see what was moving about in front of me. Just before losing interest and moving on, movement erupted as a flock of ptarmigan flushed from the low growing alders. My heart raced with the sudden surprise of sound and movement. Instinctively, I raised the revolver and aimed at one that flew directly over my head and fired. The bird dropped not ten feet behind me. Then another bunch chose to fly up and over me. With a quick aim and another rap of the firing pin, a second bird lay dead on the ground. I was extremely happy to have fresh meat, but remained puzzled as to why these birds flew up and over me; this made me think that they were not frightened by me, if so, they would have flown away from me. I reasoned that there must be something else around that had forced them into flight. My answer came quickly as I saw a lynx move stealthily through the low brush with a fat ptarmigan in his clenched jaws. If he was aware of my presence, he showed no fear or concern. For a moment, I stood in awe of what had just happened. "Two for me, one for him," I said aloud. I thanked the big tomcat for his hard work. Essentially, with a little luck on my side, he provided me with a great meal that would be fully appreciated at dinnertime.

I cleaned the birds on the spot. One thing I knew from the beginning of this adventure was that my cabin area had to remain as clean as possible in the warm months. I did not want to attract any visitors that would make life interesting and dangerous for me. I plucked the feathers rather than skinned the birds, and saved the heart, gizzard, and liver. All of these protein packed pieces of meat would be culinary pleasures at mealtime. The meat from these birds smelled fresh and clean, and in my mind, I saw them cooked and ready to eat.

I hurried back to the cabin and built a fire in the stove. The day was cooler than those I had experienced to this point, so the fire would be welcome during the night. It had been a long time since I had last eaten so making supper was the next priority. I placed my birds on a four-foot willow skewer, seasoned them with garlic, salt, and pepper, and then balanced them over the rekindled flame from the coals that remained in my fire pit.

I moved one of the chairs outside and sat by the fire as supper cooked, and occasionally rotated the skewer so as to cook the meat evenly. As I sat there I remembered a television documentary that showed a native woman cooking geese this way. It seemed a logical way to cook any type of meat. Just before the meat was done cooking, I began to think about the rest of my meal. I pushed myself up from my comfortable position and went into the cabin. I opened up a can of corn and dumped the contents in a small kettle to warm on the stove. I had some left-over noodles from the night before. In a small fry pan with some cooking oil they went, and were placed on the stove to crisp up. I sauntered back outside. Supper smelled delicious. As I sat and wondered at the beauty around me and examined the concept of freedom, my freedom, I found myself smiling at the skies. A sense of complete ease settled in the core of my being. I turned the meat one final time, stood and then walked the short distance to a knoll that overlooked the river and contemplated my place in relationship to it all—the cosmos. *Who am I, and where do I belong? How and why does a man search for his home? What makes him take the path to that home?* I smiled again because I knew I had the answers, but was, as of yet, unable to vocalize and fully appreciate my knowledge. This was good enough for me; whatever came my way, I would accept and would deal with according to the laws of nature; the consequences would be the final word.

After a few moments of contemplation, I left the knoll and trotted to the fire. Supper was done. The roasted ptarmigan with a sprinkle of added salt, the noodles and the corn were an exceptional supper. I chewed the bones clean before tossing them in the hot fire. The licking flames would kill all remaining scent. After supper, I walked to the river with axe in hand. I wanted to do a little trail work before nightfall. As I began chopping my way back to the cabin, I saw my first bear, or should I say bears. On the beach walking directly away from me at about 100 yards was a huge sow grizzly with three first year cubs. I figured her to weigh about 350 pounds and the cubs to weigh in at about 30 pounds with one being significantly smaller. The runt looked to be about 20 pounds. I watched them for a few minutes and wondered about how close they had actually come to me while I was working. The thought startled me a bit as reality set in. The sow turned once and looked straight back in my direction, but I could not tell if she was looking at the cubs or me. Regardless, it was just a bit spooky.

The four bears disappeared around the bend; I continued the chopping work on my trail but could not rid my mind of the bear sighting. A pang of anxiousness ran through me as I realized that they had probably caught wind of my flavorful supper while it was cooking, or more unnerving, while I was eating. *Were they really that close?* I thought. *I need to be more aware of my surroundings. Yes, I would have to be cautious, not fearful.* Fear was not a sense that I wanted to feel. It did not have a place in my life. Respect and awareness were what I needed for tools in this remote and wild area.

Back at the cabin, I turned to face the river. *This is great waterfront property,* I thought. After only a week here I had successfully transformed this little area into my home. It was not perfect, but the pleasing feeling about where I was at and what I could do, was incredible. I wanted for nothing more, with the exception of seeing Bill and Alvin again.

Light was fading fast, so I gathered enough dry firewood to get me through the night, re-kindled the fire in my little stove, and closed and locked the door to the cabin. I received great joy from the windows in the cabin; I could see and walk around inside at dusk with no artificial light. Each window was about thirty inches by twenty-four inches and were perfectly placed, one on the east wall and the other on the west wall. The old trapper who built this place was really thinking. The thought came to my mind: *What happened to him?* I supposed that he lost interest, or maybe got hurt and had to move back to a town or village, but my favorite thought was that he lived out his years in the wild and died somewhere in the wilderness, never to be found. It was a good thought, one that I wished for myself when I became an old man. The day had been long and a lot of work had been done. I laid down to rest. Sleep came quickly.

Chapter 15
Too Close to the Cabin

My eyes opened slowly; *had I heard a sound or was I dreaming? No, there it was again! Is it in here? Outside?* My senses were on high alert as I lay motionless in my bed. After a few moments, I reached for my 30-06. It was loaded and ready. The bears that I saw the night before were on the top of my mind. Slowly, I lifted myself from my bed and moved toward the east window. With the rifle in the ready position, I pinned my face against the window pane and looked as far down both sides of the window as I could see, nothing. I glanced quickly at my watch. It was 4:45am. The sound started again. It was a rustle emanating from the direction of the fire pit. I could not see the area from either window, but knew it was the bears.

I waited for a long time by the window facing east in hopes that whatever was making the noise would move around so I could identify what it was. My heart was pounding in my chest as I crept over to the other window. Right when I got there, I was met eyeball to eyeball with a gigantic grizzly bear that rose up and stared in at me. We startled each other; he woofed and ran while I simultaneously screamed like a child who had seen a ghost, and jumped back to the center of the cabin. My heart was pounding harder. I heard him rip through the alders and when I moved back to the window, saw the brush swish over his back on his way to the river. He was running parallel to my trail, and when he hit the beach area, I caught a glimpse of him as he turned right and headed upstream. In seconds, all was eerily quiet. Still, I stood without moving for several minutes, all the while expecting the bear to return.

After I settled down and realized the bear was not hunting me, rather he was doing what bears do, scavenging for food, being a bear, I felt better. It was Incidents like this that grew my respect for this vast and wild land and all of its inhabitants. If I was to be successful here, I would have to take certain precautions. That is the way of life in the wild. Eventually I calmed down and went about my morning business.

As a result of the bear sightings from the last two days I became anxious to clear the alders further out in all directions from my cabin. This would give me reaction time for any bear approaching my home. I reminded myself that this was common sense, not fear.

So, that is what I did. I spent the day chopping hundreds of alders and dragging them to the cabin area where they would dry over time. To speed up the drying process, I fired up the chainsaw and cut the alders into eighteen-inch pieces that would fit in the stove and work well for a quick fire in the fire pit.

I finished my firewood work, and even though it was late in the day, I decided to pick the blueberries that were hanging heavily on the bushes waiting to be picked and canned. The idea of canning the berries produced some anxiety in me since this would be my first attempt at preserving my winter food. I felt lucky that I had some of the modern items that the old timers did not have. I thought about how hard it would have been to keep berries and other foods through the winter without spoilage.

Still in thought, I unpacked one of my pressure canners and one of my turkey cookers, along with a canister of propane. After everything was set up, I read the instructions for both and felt confident that this would not be a difficult task to complete. After gaining this knowledge on the subject I became energized and excited. I grabbed my rifle and some pails and headed off to pick berries.

The berries were ripe, and some were already past their prime. I picked two huge pails of blueberries, and figured I had about thirty pints of fruit. I trudged back to the cabin with my heavy load. Then I grabbed two five-gallon pails and went to the river for some clean water. I needed three quarts of water for the pressure canner, and a little bit for each jar so I would have enough liquid in each one to produce a rich berry juice that could be thickened into a syrup. I put the three quarts of water in the canner as required, and after cleaning the jars and filling them with berries, added a half-cup of water and a couple tablespoons of sugar to each. After that was done, I placed a lid on each jar and tightened them down by screwing the lid tightly in place.

I had thirty-seven pints of berries and began to can them nine jars at a time. The pressure canner was not hard to use, but it did require my entire attention in order to keep the pressure at ten pounds. As I found out through trial and error, any adjustment to the flame under the canner, had to be done in tiny increments or else the pressure would change rapidly.

The first batch was done so I turned off the flame and let the pressure canner cool. After about ten minutes, the pressure seal on the canner lid dropped signifying that all of the pressure inside the canner had been depleted. I unlocked the cover and removed it. I saw the canned berries. This was a first-time experience for me. They were beautiful in their dark purple syrup, and I knew they would taste like a warm summer day poured over my winter pancakes. I continued my work, and as each batch cooled, I placed the jars back in their original boxes and shoved them under the bed for storage. This way they would be out of the way and I could pull out a jar whenever I wanted one.

Finally, I was done with the canning project. The job had lasted deep into the night, but I was happy that it was completed for the year. I hoped that thirty-seven pints was enough to get me through the winter and spring. The day's work had exhausted me. It was time for bed. My rest was badly needed as I had much planned for the next day.

Chapter 16
Scouting my Trapping Area

I opened my eyes in the early morning light and immediately remembered my planned scouting trip. Excitement gripped me. Without hesitation, I jumped out of bed and packed up food and sleeping gear, enough for two days. I made a big bowl of oatmeal for breakfast and topped it with a pile of brown sugar and some left-over blueberries that I kept for fresh eating. When the dishes were washed and all my things were sitting out by the fire pit ready to go, I pulled the door shut as I walked out, picked up my pack, my axe, and my .30-06. As usual, my .22 pistol was securely strapped to my hip.

This would be a long trip, and a journey into woods and land that I had never before laid eyes on. I was excited and my hands shook with anticipation. I decided to go to the river and head upstream through a thick growth of spruce that looked like it should hold a great many marten. Marten have a highly sought-after fur and are quite easy to catch. Well, at least that is what my trapping books told me. As I walked along the riverbank, I began to see tracks going into the water and then coming out of the water in a different spot a short way upstream. I bent down to examine them more clearly, and discovered the tracks to be those of a beaver. I had not anticipated seeing this sign, but was very happy to come across it in what was considered my backyard. Bill had mentioned earlier in the year that beaver prices were expected to be high, so this made trapping them a worthwhile pursuit.

It was too early in the year to have trapping fever, but there it was nagging at me well before the pelts would be prime and ready for harvesting. My goal was to not use any more of my inherited money than was needed. Rather, I wanted to catch all sorts of fur bearing animals and sell them in order to maintain my life in the wilderness. Hunting for my meat and picking berries created no problem in my thinking, but having a supply of flour, salt, sugar, coffee, oatmeal, and spices, along with other small items would take money. It became clear that trapping would be my only income for these essential items.

After examining the tracks for a bit, I turned and jumped up on some fallen logs that leaned against the bank. With my free hand, I pulled myself upright into a wonderful stand of spruce trees. Immediately I saw marten scat on the ground in front of me. The trapping fever went a notch higher. The spruce grove went high up the steep hillside, and as I followed it upward found that the marten sign littered the ground. About halfway up the mountain, the spruce grove ended and alders took over. Further up beyond the alders, the ground was barren. I could not help but think that this was a trapper's paradise.

In the alders, I found rabbit turds, and, to my pleasant surprise, lynx waste. These findings sent me into a frenzy of thinking how lucky I was to have chosen this spot, although quite randomly, not as random as throwing a dart at a map and going off to live in the spot where the dart landed. Yet it did incorporate that basic philosophy, along with some map research, some help from Bill and Alvin, and some common sense thrown in. I knew before coming here that I would need to be relatively close to civilization if I wanted to take advantage of selling my furs and buying products that I needed. For certain, I knew that I did not want any unneeded interference from the outside world. This did not include meeting up with another trapper or an occasional hunter. I thought back to how I ran away from the rat race that is modern society; it was not for me, but, like I said, the occasional visitor would be welcomed.

As I reached the top of the mountain, which is not an actual mountain, just a very big hill with jagged outcroppings in places and a relatively smooth and rounded top, I found it the perfect place for lunch. Climbing in this terrain is hard work. As I rifled through my backpack for some food, I realized that I needed to prepare much better for these excursions. This was my first outing and already I knew the food I brought with me would not be enough. I think I was following my natural tendency for preserving things, and had probably packed light foodstuff in an attempt to ration my food supply. But, as I thought about it more, I realized it was getting close to the time when I could shoot a moose or caribou and not have it spoil on me. Even though I had jars and a pressure canner, I would wait; I did not want to waste a beautiful animal to rot and flies just because I could not process it fast enough.

The food I had with me would have to do. I built a small fire out of dried grasses and small twigs. It was enough to warm my lunch. After eating my sugar-sweetened cornmeal porridge, I stood up, repacked my backpack, snuffed out the fire, and then proceeded down the backside of this super-sized hill. Eventually, I re-entered the line of alders and then the spruce trees as I descended. On the backside near the bottom I heard water running over rocks. I stopped and listened for a moment, and then after closing most of the distance, I noticed that the sound of water emanated from a small stream running down the hill. It made a sharp bend and then continued to run parallel with the base of the hill. As I thought about this, I reasoned that it would meet up with the river someplace downstream from my cabin. If this worked out as I thought it would, running the trap line would be easier and safer with the creek as a guide.

I continued my journey as I followed the water downhill. It did not take long for me to find the spot where the creek made confluence with my river. *Sweet,* I thought, *this will serve me well!* As I turned and faced upstream I thought that I could faintly make out the remnants of my woodpile. The river was straight here, and I figured I could see a mile upstream. That meant I had probably walked a total of 5 miles, and that would be a great trap line for my first year. I leaned my rifle against a tree stump that had washed up to the cut bank and then turned to look downstream. "Bear!" The word emitted from my lips in a low but forceful whisper.

Chapter 17
This Could Be a Problem

She was a monster, surrounded closely by three alert, rust colored cubs, one a runt. *These are the same bears I saw by the cabin,* I thought. Her stare was dead on me, eyes locked in place. I had never seen a bear this close before. I noticed immediately that there was a much different sensation rolling around in my gut from the feeling I first had when I saw her on the beach by my cabin.

Fear pulsed in my veins. I could not help it. I was in trouble. I could have sworn that I looked downstream before I walked completely out of the trees. I could not recall seeing anything out of the ordinary on the beach, but there she was, less than fifty feet from me, too close for comfort. Realizing the danger of my situation, I slowly reached for my rifle, and as I did, she broke into a full-blown charge. I moved fast to retrieve my rifle, but was not quick enough. She hit me in what seemed like a fraction of a second, the force of the collision knocked my gun out of my hand. Her powerful head and jaws felt like boulders rolling past me as she side-swiped my body. I was not knocked down because she veered off course at the last fraction of a second. I did not understand why she did this. Was she warning me that I had gotten too close? Rotted fish and dank water smell filled the air and my senses felt the assault. My hand hurt badly. I looked down and saw my little finger dangling from a small piece of skin and meat; the bone was completely broken.

The bear stopped but did not turn back toward me; she stood there panting and grunting like a spoiled child not wanting to face his punishing mother, her chest and stomach heaving with each agitated breath. I turned slowly and quietly to face her. I did not know her intentions, but could hear the cubs snapping their jaws and wailing a few yards behind me. This was the absolutely worst position to be in. I wished the cubs had run off to safety. Fear built in me, and I became angry with myself for not paying attention to my surroundings. My mind raced with the thoughts of my recklessness. If I lived through this, I would have to make changes in how I participated in this wild land. For a moment, time seemed to stand still.

Then, like someone pressed the start button on a stopwatch, the big sow slowly turned to face me. I felt as if I was in an old western cowboy movie where one gunfighter calls another out to the street for a pistol showdown, where only one will survive. Then, again, for a fleeting second, it felt as if we were locked in time, eye to eye, where everything stood still, one waiting for the other to draw. Then movement, as the cubs began to scurry about, still chomping their teeth. The old sow stood her ground, no movement, not a blink of an eye.

Survival meant that I had to get my .30-06 off the ground. The pistol strapped to my hip, I thought, would do nothing but add a dose of anger to the beast's already elevated sense of perturbation. *My rifle, my rifle,* like a broken record, kept playing in my mind. Slowly, as to not make any sharp movements, I bent sharply at the waist and in full stretch, narrowly reached the weapon. I gently fingered my gun in an attempt to pull it closer. The bear reacted slightly to the noise of the gun rustling on the rocks and sand. But when I was raising the rifle to my shoulder, the scraping of cloth on the butt end of my gun as it rubbed my jacket drove her mad. She made quick and determined steps toward me, but did not come on a run, just a steady and determined amble. I clicked the safety off and aimed at her gigantic head and pulled the trigger. Nothing! The bolt was not all the way down, leaving the chambered round useless.

Before I could close the chamber and attempt to fire again, her rage was boiling over as she leaned into a full charge. The big bear hit me with a force that seemed to shake the ground I stood on. All in the same charging motion she delivered a powerful swat that hit my shoulder and deflected from there to the side of my head. With a huge paw and enormous claws, she rendered me helpless. I was thrust to the ground. The one-two punch dazed me for a few seconds. As I regained some of my senses, I smelled her fish breath rifle through my nostrils. Pain racked my body and the blood in my eyes darkened the day and gave me the sense that this was the end of my life. I saw my little cabin in my mind's eye, and briefly thought of my friends, Bill and Alvin. I passed out.

When I came to, she was standing over me with one of her front paws resting lightly just under my chin, the sharp claws biting into my neck. The other mammoth paw with its enormous claws was resting heavily on my right arm. I tried to squirm from beneath the beast but my arm was securely pinned to the ground. She was treating me like a toy and it hurt. She bounced up and down, and on the downward thrust came chest to chest with me, leaving no escape options. My mind slowly came back to the surface after the initial impact. I had to make my move or accept the fact that I would die out here covered in mud and blood. My decision was made. I reached for my pistol, drew it from the holster, and slowly raised it to a point under her chin that seemed to line up with her brain and then let the Smith and Wesson rip. Round after round went inside the limits of her lower jaws and hopefully into her monstrous head. It was a surreal event as it happened. I heard the gunshots. I saw her standing over me, motionless, like a huge boulder that even the biggest bulldozers would not be able to budge. It all happened so quickly. I did not know for sure if all the lead had met its mark in the beast's head, and did not know if any real damage had been done. After what seemed like days had passed, she turned and ran thunderously into the spruce and alders with frightening ferocity. She was gone. All was quiet.

After a long time of intent listening for even the tiniest crack of a twig, I worked up the courage to make a move. I carefully rolled to my side and searched the ascending slope for sign of the bear. Nothing! I found the pocket in my jacket that held the spare ammunition and re-loaded my pistol, all the while keeping a keen eye in the direction that she ran. As my breathing slowed to a normal pace and my bearing became clear, I felt pain in my hands and realized my finger was no longer attached, lost somewhere in the rocks and mud. The nub where my little finger used to be attached was coagulated with sand, blood, and mud; the bleeding had stopped. I hoped that was a sign that the wound would heal without an infection setting in. For now, however, the finger was the least of my worries.

Slowly and painfully, I sat up and worked my way to the standing position. I felt completely worn out and dizzy. There was no sign of the bear. I looked around for my rifle and found it thirty feet away partially submerged in river water. The impact of the bear hitting me head on was impressive. After a short and fast-paced examination, I was relieved to find that there was not a lot more damage to my body. There was blood in my hair and on my face, but I could not feel any gaping wounds.

As I stood there, further gaining my composure, the pain in my body began to subside. It was replaced with anger directed toward myself. I would now have to find this bear, probably wounded, maybe dead. The cubs, if she were dead, would have to fend for themselves. I feared that they would succumb to predation or the winter cold. My heart sank. Either way, the task of locating this bear was a daunting one.

I retrieved my rifle from where it lay and cleaned it as thoroughly as ten seconds allowed, then turned and fired a shot into the river. It worked. I ejected that round and locked the bolt down tight. I turned and scanned the hillside through the alders and under the spruce trees. There she was. I saw the big sow eyeing me from a spot where she was partially concealed by a fallen tree trunk and some alder brush. I could not get a clean shot from the beach, so I worked my way inside the wood line and stealthily closed the distance between us. I needed to get a killing shot before she charged again.

The bear made no movement as I inched through the woods. I inadvertently cracked some twigs, and noticed that she did not move. Nothing! No sign of life! I stopped; I could have taken a shot that insured the bear would be dead, but something compelled me to go closer. I hoped it was not a death wish on my part.

At twenty feet I saw the bear blink. Simultaneously her body shuddered as if she were attempting to charge me, with no real movement materializing. In her bullet riddled control center, the brain said charge, but the connection to the muscles was damaged, which left the great beast paralyzed. I knew now that one or more of the .22 caliber rounds had lodged in her brain rendering the bear incapable of doing me any more damage. I felt a great sense of relief.

I dropped to one knee fully intending to shoot the bear dead, yet I stopped, lowered the rifle, and then apologized to her. The apology was not for taking her life; rather the apology was for the circumstances that I created, that resulted in her death. I pressed my human wants upon a critter with no such desire. I saw this as a human incident, not a bear incident. My actions saddened me.

After vowing to know better the land and beasts around me, I raised the gun, made a heart-felt apology, and then killed the bear with one shot to the head. Only then did I notice the small and fragile runt cub cupped inside her front legs. The other two were nowhere to be seen or heard.

For many reasons I was not happy. I was missing a finger, and in front of me lay a massive dead bear and a tiny cub, blinking its small black eyes at me. I would deal with the finger at the cabin, but for now, there were other chores that needed doing. I did not have a lot of experience skinning animals, so this would be a new job to learn. I knew that saving the meat and making use of it was important. With the butt of my rifle, and not without a considerable resistance from the cub, I finally forced it to leave its mother's side. After a few seconds of biting and wrestling the stock of my gun it darted about twenty feet into the brush and curled up by a fallen log, all the while snarling and hissing its disapproval of my presence. I knew I would have to do something with the cub if it hung around, instead of what I really hoped for, its reuniting with its birth-mates. I immediately began the task of skinning the bear. My knife was sharp and it glided easily through the skin. The work agitated my wounds and my whole body began to ache again. The throbbing in my hand reminded me that I was now minus a little finger. There was nothing else to do but continue the job in front of me.

I made quick work of removing the hide; I figured my speed was due to the high levels of adrenaline still flowing, like a raging river, through my body. The first thing I noticed once the hide was free from the body, was its weight. I rolled it up as tightly as possible and tied it snuggly with rope that was always in my pack. I left several feet of rope dangling after the knot was tied. This would help me hold it high on my back for the trip home. After removing my axe from its place in my backpack, I chopped the four quarters off of the bear and laid them beneath the nearby trees. As I worked, I watched for the return of the other two bear cubs. There was no sign of them, and the runt cub never moved from the spot it had scurried to. Even with the high degree of sadness I felt over this occurrence, I was glad that I had studied my outdoor living books. Reading them taught me how to do the work I was now engaged in. Without gutting the bear, I took the back straps and the hide and headed home. I would return in the morning and make a couple more trips for the remainder of the meat. The initial anger I felt over this incident had waned, in its place was the worry for the little runt cub. That little cub was all I could think about on the long and painful walk to the cabin.

Chapter 18
Patchwork and Rest

With my aching and battered body still mostly intact, I finally arrived back at the cabin. My first priority was to hang the bear hide on the sunny side of the cabin. The sun had been shining for days, and the air was dry. I hoped that this warm dry weather would continue. I did not have the best equipment available to hang and stretch the huge and heavy hide. After walking around and pondering how to get this job done, a thought popped in my head. I grabbed a spruce pole that was about ten feet long and placed it under the hide running parallel to the long side of the skin. After the pole was in place, I folded the edge of the fur side back over the pole so that fur touched fur, exposing the inside of the hide to the sun and wind. I allowed enough hide to lap over so that holes could be punched through it and when tied securely together the spruce pole would act as a hanger. Then I tied rope to both ends of the pole and hoisted one end up to the rough-hewn rafter ends of the cabin and tied it in place. I did the same thing to the other end of the pole. This left the hide inches off the ground, and that was perfect. While I was still dirty, I cut and scraped the fat off of the hide, and then took some old nails I had saved and loosely nailed parts of the hide to the cabin wall so that it would maintain its shape as it dried. Just before I was ready to clean up, I rubbed in a heavy dose of salt to the inside of the hide to help the drying process.

This was not tanning the hide, but it would function for my needs. I was much happier now that I had the majority of the work done. I wanted to make sure that everything from the bear would be used. I did not like wasting things. As I was thinking about frying bear steaks for supper, I felt a twinge of pain in my hand and a hurt in my heart for the lonely cub. With all the excitement, I had, until now, forgotten about losing my finger.

Since it was relatively warm, I stripped down to my birthday suit, and then embarrassingly looked around for gawkers before realizing where I was. This made me laugh. I was free. I grabbed my soap and an old towel that I almost did not pack, and gingerly picked my way to the river. The water was cold and instantly made me shiver. As I washed, I found it difficult to get the soap film off of my skin. With harsh rubbing and a lot of fresh water slapped on my skin, it finally came off and I felt clean. I then turned my attention to my throbbing hand where my finger used to connect to it. It had begun to bleed again. I could see the cleanly sliced bone and the jagged pieces of flesh hanging in small strands from my hand. It looked like my finger had gone through a meat saw in a butcher shop. Apparently, the bear had caught me with a tooth, and maybe clamped down on it too. I honestly did not remember how the whole scene played out. I vigorously washed the wound even though it hurt like the dickens. In my pack there was a bottle of iodine that I bought along at the urging of Bill. Iodine is a disinfectant, and it would come in handy on this open wound. I finished up at the river and, in a hurried pace, made my way back to the cabin. By the time I got there I was shivering violently and it made it hard to grasp and turn the door handle. Once inside the cabin, I did my best to rip an old shirt into shreds and then used one piece as a temporary band aide. After the bleeding began to subside, I took a fingernail clipper and cut off the ragged pieces of skin and then dabbed iodine on the wound and wrapped it snuggly in a piece of the shirt, tucking the ends beneath the wrap, holding the bandage in place. I drank a couple quarts of water, and then lay down on my bed and covered up with every blanket that I had. My hand and my body were sore and I was tired like I had never been tired before. The throbbing was easing up and eventually I stopped shivering. The pain had subsided to a dull ache. I slept.

Chapter 19
Recovery and Loss

I awoke to bright sunshine coming through my windows. I could tell it was the middle of the day. I did not feel any pain until I moved in an attempt to raise myself from my bunk. Immediately, I relaxed back into my comfortable bed. As I lay there thinking, my stomach grumbled. It was awakening to the fact that I had not eaten since yesterday afternoon. That was twenty-four hours and a bear attack ago. Needless to say, I was hungry. I forced myself up, found a can of stew and poured it in a pan and placed it on the stove. That is when I realized that I had no fire. I turned and lit the Coleman stove and put the pan of stew on that to warm up. I was going to light a fire in the woodstove, but it felt comfortable in the cabin, so I let that go undone for the time being.

My hand and body still hurt enough to remind me of the bear attack. My mind drifted back to the scene that had rapidly and violently unfolded the day before. After a few minutes in thought, I heard the stew hit the boiling point, snapping me out of my dream-like remembrance as it hissed and sent flying drops of broth on the pan above the line where the liquid filled the hot container. I turned the flame off to allow the stew to cool, and then began to examine my hand. As I unwrapped the bandage, I could see that a splotch of blood the size of a grapefruit had soaked into the old shirt, but had since stopped. Because there was not a solid scab on the wound I dipped iodine on it and allowed it to dry in the open air while I ate lunch. The hot stew made me tired so I crawled back in bed to rest and think about recovering the bear meat. *I will have to get up soon,* I thought, *the meat will spoil. What about the cub. The cub.* My mind drifted to the kill site. I figured since I already had the hide here, it would only take two trips to get the bear meat back to the cabin. My plan was to cut up and can as many quarts as possible and then roast some for fresh eating. Thinking about the meat reminded me that I had brought the back straps home with me the night before. Slowly, I raised myself out of bed and took a whiff of the meat; it smelled good so I went back to bed. I was tired and only remember a moment of thought after my head hit the pillow. I did not know how many days I had slept, but when I woke up, it was early morning, and a heavy rain was falling. The wind was blowing hard. My thoughts went to the bear meat and the cub. I had to make a recovery effort and several worries and questions plagued my mind. *Would the cub still be there, or would they all be there?*

As I began moving around in bed, trying to stretch wounded and inactive muscles, I noticed that I did not feel well. There was only a little pain in my hand, and none in my body or head; however, I was very stiff. At first, it was extremely hard to move. Finally, I sat up and looked around the cabin; it was cold. I felt nauseated. I moved to the stove and opened the door to fill it with wood. In minutes, I had a nice fire built and burning. A couple minutes later I had oatmeal water boiling. I added oatmeal and raisins and waited for it to be ready to eat. When it finished cooking, I added brown sugar and molasses.

I realized that my hunger was overwhelming; as soon as my two bowls of oatmeal were devoured, I felt better. The nauseating sensation I had experienced was gone and I once again felt strong. I was amazed at how my hand looked without its fifth appendage. It appeared alien to me. Although still puffy from the injury, and well bruised and red, the wound seemed to be healing. I had never known a person who was missing a part of his body. This was an odd feeling.

From the breakfast table to the bed I went, but not for more sleep. I could tell that my body had all the rest it needed for the time being. Sitting on the edge, I fully cleaned my pistol and my 30-06. Both had taken a considerable beating during the bear attack and needed a thorough inspection and clean up. After completing the work on my guns, I decided that target practice was required before making the journey back for the bear kill site.

I dressed in warm clothes and eagerly slipped on my Muck boots. I donned my rain gear, grabbed my 30-06, the .22 pistol, and a box of ammunition for each. Outside the cabin I had set up a target shooting range that was nothing special to see, but provided me with everything I needed to keep my guns finely tuned. The fresh oil on the rifle barrel made the rainwater bead up and balance precariously on the barrel's rounded top. The rain had slowed to a drizzle, yet it would completely soak me in an hour or so without my rain gear. Sighting the rifle took several shots; the scope took a hard blow, but did not break anything. That was amazing to me. After fifteen minutes or so the job was done, both guns were spot on in terms of accuracy. With all my needed equipment, I headed down the beach to recover the bear meat, which I had come to realize was probably devoured by wolves, or rotten. The cub dominated my thinking. I simply could not get that little bear off my mind.

Chapter 20
Cabin Partner

As I had figured, the warmth and the rain spoiled the bear meat. My heart sank. I had just wasted a beautiful animal. *Maybe four,* I thought. The anger I felt toward myself resurfaced as the smell of the rotted flesh assaulted my nostrils, but reality is reality, the meat was unusable. My mind quickly switched to thinking about the runt bear cub. I walked to where I had last seen it. To my amazement, there it lay, motionless. Dead. I almost threw up. I was so upset with myself that I could barely come to terms with what I was seeing. At this point, the only thing I could do was bury it along with the remains of its mother.

I pulled my pack shovel out and tossed it to the spot where I would dig a burial hole, and then turned to pick up the tiny cub. It moved! It's not dead! Ever so slightly, it moved! My heart jumped. I scooped the cub up like it was a long-lost teddy bear from my youth. I didn't know what the future held for this tiny, fragile bear, but I knew I would do everything in my power to help it live. With my arms gently but tightly wrapped around its tiny frame, holding it close to my chest, I sprinted home through the now driving, cold rain.

I had never run that hard before and even though I had worked up to a full sweat and felt overheated, I was thankful for the warm, dry cabin. I charged into the cabin and gently laid the little bear next to the stove. She was shivering. It was a little female cub. This was the first time I saw it as more than a bear cub; it was a little she-bear. My heart raced with excitement as my mind considered all the possibilities of having a bear. *As a pet*, I thought. *Is that possible.* Well, first I had to save her life, which I had come so close to snuffing out. I was fumbling about the cabin looking for something that would nourish my little bear. After a few false excitements over a possible remedy, I remembered that I packed a couple boxes of dried milk. Bill had told me that it would come in handy for making pancakes and biscuits. I found the dried milk in a crate under my bed, then quickly read the directions on the box and thought the mixture would be too weak to help my little bear. I grabbed a quart jar and filled it half full of water and then added an extra quarter cup of dried milk to the water than was called for. With shaking fingers, I screwed the lid on the jar and shook the lidded container vigorously until the flakes were thoroughly dissolved, and then put it on the stovetop in a shallow pan of water. The milk had to be warmed up, this I knew because the mother's milk would always be warm. While the milk was on the stove, I turned my attention back to my little friend who was still shivering on the floor. I grabbed a towel and gently dried her hair. Slowly and delicately, my little bear opened her eyes; she showed no sign of resistance, but then she was as close to death as a living creature could be. I wrapped her in another towel that was dry and then tucked my pillow under her head and upper body. I reached for the milk. It was warm.

She perked up just a little bit when I brought the milk close and took the lid off the jar. The little bear made soft grunts and snorts as if to tell me that I was not mamma, but that I would do in this situation. There was no question that she was hungry and needed nourishment. At first the little cub resisted every way I tried to get milk in her mouth. As a last resort, I smeared some on her nose and immediately afterward, put a milky finger in her mouth. She made a sucking motion so I repeated this until she accepted milk that I had poured in the palm of my hand. From that point on she consumed the remaining milk by lapping it out of my hand. Each time she licked my hand clean, I added more milk for her to lap up. The sight made me laugh because the little bear was on her side, one watchful, mistrusting eye on me and the other hungry eye on the milk and hand as she struggled to lift her head and drink the warm, nourishing milk.

After consuming the milk, she still seemed to be hungry, and the thought of what to feed her challenged me. I had heard that a person should never over-feed an animal that has been without food for a long time, or in this case, starving. I knew that the bear would naturally be eating some solid food at this age. Blueberries were just out of season, yet most likely a favorite in the bear world. I got up and grabbed a pint of canned berries and popped the lid off. My little bear cub livened up just a bit more when she heard the sound. She seemed stronger, and began to chomp her teeth at me in a half-hearted attempt to tell me she was a dangerous bear. I smiled at her as I lowered myself to her side with a few berries in my hand. Now, both of her eyes were on the food, not me. I allowed her to eat half of the berries and half of the juice. As she ate, I could tell that her breathing was less laborious and that she had stopped shivering.

It was getting chilly in the cabin so I stood up and opened the stove door. She did not like this and shakily scurried away on four very weak legs to an open area just under a corner of my bunk where I had pulled the box out that held the canned berries. She made a couple grunt noises and chomped her teeth warning me to watch what I do. I laughed a bit at her little displays of toughness, as I verbally assured her that she was in charge. She curled up there and went to sleep. I could not tell whether she trusted me or if she was too tired and weak to do anything else. I quietly finished stoking up the stove and then gently shut the door.

I sat down at the table and watched the sleeping cub. I found it hard to take my eyes off of the sleeping little bear, but once again, I noticed that my hand was throbbing. I had bumped it several times beginning back when I picked up the little bear and ran home with her. To make matters worse, while stoking the stove I caught it between a chunk of wood and the side of the stove door frame. It made me wince in pain, and now I could tell it was bleeding. I slowly unwrapped my hand. The skin on my hand was all kinds of colors ranging from blue to a sickening looking yellow. Blood was running down my wrist and onto my arm. I grabbed a piece of the shirt that was ripped in shreds for bandages and wiped my arm clean. Since the wound was open, I doused it again with iodine and wrapped it snuggly. It hurt quite a bit, but I could see that it was not infected. That was a good thing; if it were infected I would have been in big trouble and in need of medical attention, so I felt lucky at this point.

While the little bear slept, hunger pangs hit me full force. I opened a can of stew and warmed it in the can on the stovetop. The food satisfied me. While eating, I realized it was a good time to go back to the dead bear and finish what I started. I did not want to leave the cub alone, but really had no choice. I thought about how to care for her while I was gone and eventually decided to pour the rest of the blueberries and their juice in the stew can and put it on the floor by the stove. As an afterthought before heading out the door, I stirred in a couple teaspoons of powdered milk. If the little bear woke up while I was gone, she would have something to eat and hopefully that would keep her occupied in my absence.

It had quit raining, but I took my rain gear just in case. It was chilly in the late afternoon. Both guns were loaded and ready, the pistol on my hip and the rifle slung over my shoulder. The walk down to the bear was peaceful. It felt good to be moving again with reduced stress in me over the bear incident. I took time to enjoy my surroundings and noticed that fish were nosing up out in the river, but could not tell what they were. I promised myself that I would do some fishing tomorrow.

My pack and shovel were just as I had left them. I picked up the shovel and began my task. Digging in the soft ground was not difficult except for the occasional spruce root that was inconveniently placed. With considerable effort, I cut through the roots and once the grave was deep enough, I carried the bear parts to the hole and gently laid them to rest. I do not know exactly why, but I promised the old sow bear that I would take care of her baby, and that I would look for the two other cubs and do what I could to make sure they were not starving. A gentle thought came to me that said, *all three of her cubs would be fine*. I hoped so.

After finishing my solemn duties at the gravesite and packing up my tools, I loaded the pack on my back, shouldered the rifle, and took one last look at the area. With that I walked up the hill and along the little gurgling stream. I made several circles, each one wider than the other in search for the bear cubs; there was no sign of them. Because of their size I believed they would do fine on their own. It was getting late, so I headed for the cabin, glad that this episode was over with.

I approached my cabin as quietly as possible so as not to surprise and frighten the little bear cub that I hoped was still resting, but as I got closer, I realized it did not matter; my little bear was not sleeping. I could hear a scraping sound that made me think she was pushing the stew can across the cabin floor. A peek in the window confirmed my thought. I moved to the door and began to slowly open it. The little bear heard the door and had apparently recovered enough to stand up on her hind legs and chomp her teeth at me. She probably thought she was displaying a terrifying ferocity that would scare me away. I stood in the doorway for a moment watching as she frantically sniffed the air trying to figure out exactly what I was. After a short re-acquaintance deliberation, she seemed to recognize my scent, then lowered herself to all fours and retreated to her area under the corner of my bunk. I chuckled to myself at her toughness. She was tiny, but certainly knew her inherent place in the animal kingdom.

"Hey little girl," I said in a soft and soothing voice as I walked into the cabin. "Did you enjoy your snack?" I rambled on as if she could understand me." I buried your mamma and looked for your sibling cubs, but could not find them. I think they will be fine. I believe you and I are partners now. What do you think about that?"

She lay in her spot, and with a quizzical look in her eyes, watched my every move. She reminded me of a dog we had when I was a small boy. He would lie for long periods of time simply tracking the movements around him. In this case the little bear's eyes followed me as I tracked back and forth across the cabin floor.

Partners, I thought. H*ow the heck am I going to take care of a bear? Will she hibernate? We are well into September. Winter is close. What the heck am I going to do with this little bear cub?*
"What do you think little girl, do you want to be my partner out here?"
I already knew the answer to my question. She was my responsibility for as long as she needed me. After all, I killed her mother, and though I did not see killing a bear as a bad thing, it happened to be a bear with three cubs. I was sure the other two would be okay, but this little girl would surely die without my help.

This incident, as time went by, taught me some things about life in the wild. Heck, who am I trying to kid, it taught me everything about life. I learned that my actions always have reactions. The consequences of my actions can be fortunate, or they can be unfortunate. This one seemed to be a mixture of both.

Lesson learned. *I need to name this bear and get to know her,* I thought as I considered her supper and mine. She seemed ready for some solid food, so I whipped up a double batch of pancakes and made syrup out of brown sugar, white sugar, and water. After boiling this mixture for a few minutes, it was a thick and rich syrup that would be great on our cakes. The smells in the cabin activated the little bear's senses. She poked her nose in and out of one of my boots that was lying on the floor by the stove. She seemed to sense that something good was coming, but waited patiently for supper to be served. She looked so cute with her nose in the boot and those black eyes showing effort to figure out all of the new smells around her.

Pretty Girl, I thought. Then I said it out loud, "Pretty Girl". It sounded good. The name fit her. From that point on her name was Pretty Girl. "Hey, Pretty Girl, do you want some pancakes and syrup?" I answered for her. "Of course, you do! Well, here they are."

I sat on the floor next to the stove and placed her plate of food on the floor beside me. She did not move from her spot by the boots across from me. Her nose was free and could smell the goodies waiting for her. She was hungry, but not real eager to eat next to me. Just like a human being, however, the drive to fill an empty stomach is powerful. She slowly crawl-walked and growl-snarled her way to the plate and began licking the syrup off of the cakes. Soon she was gobbling the goodies, as was I. I guess we were both hungrier than I thought. Slowly, I raised my free hand and placed it on her back and gently began to stroke her hide. Pretty Girl gave notice by making a couple soft growls but did not snap at me or pull away, and certainly did not miss a bite of food. I hoped this was a display of trust and not simply the need to eat that gave me permission to pet her. We had not been together for very long, but I seemed to sense in her that she did not see me as a danger. I hoped that was the case.

It was late when I pushed myself up from the floor. Pretty girl had long since moved to her spot under the bunk. I had spent more than an hour sitting and watching her as I contemplated my time so far at my cabin home.

Yes, cabin home, I thought. *The place I want to be.* Time was moving quickly and things I could never have guessed would happen did happen. Essentially, I became a parent in the first month of my new life on my own.

"Hey Pretty Girl," I said, "It is time for bed." I gathered some wood and stoked the fire, then opened the door to feel the night air. It was cold, and I thought I smelled snow in the air. It was too early for snow to fall and stay, but not too early for a snowfall. I was excited for winter because that meant my first year of hunting and trapping would be here.

As excited as I was for all of that to begin, it was squelched to some extent because I

had so much worry on my mind for Pretty Girl. Tomorrow, I thought, I will dig a den on the hillside just up from the cabin, well out of reach from any potential floodwaters. I hoped that this would serve as my bear's hibernation den. The spot would give me the ability to keep the den clearly in view from one window and from the door of the cabin. As I surveyed the situation, I concluded that just because she would be in hibernation did not mean she was safe.

I closed the cabin door, slipped out of my boots and pants, and gave a quick look at Pretty Girl. She was fast asleep. I lit a candle, turned off the lantern, and crawled into bed; it had been a long day. Sleep came quickly.

Chapter 21
Building A Second Home

I woke up to the sound of scratching. Scratching, and the now familiar grunts and snorts. It was Pretty Girl. She was trying to claw through the wall right next to the door. Automatically, I deduced that she wanted to go outside. Not knowing what to expect, I got up and walked to the door talking to her the entire time. I opened the door wide in one swing. She did not hesitate to take advantage of the opening. The cub bear was an image of lightning as she bolted through the door space. I watched her run toward the river and became worried that she would go and not come back. My heart sank. I got dressed and stepped into the cold damp day; I thought to myself, *it would snow before nightfall.* After throwing on some clothes and a jacket and with my 30-06 in my hand, I trotted to the river and scanned the banks in both directions. She was not there. Back in the area of the cabin I searched, eyes strained, all of the open areas but could see nothing out of the ordinary. After a bit more time, the thought came to me that if I made breakfast she would come running to the smell of food. She did not. My heart sank to a deeper depth of despair. I sat outside in the cold and ate fried spam wrapped in a pancake made from batter the night before.

After breakfast I grabbed my shovel and rifle and climbed the side hill to the right of my cabin. I had not given up my hope for Pretty Girl's safe return, so I went forth with the den project. Once there I picked a spot that was visible from my doorway and visible from one window and started digging into the earth. The ground was cold but not frozen. This was not far enough north for the permafrost to be close to the surface. Digging was hard, and before long, I felt the pangs of hunger rumbling in my belly. I wanted fish, so I dropped what I was doing and went back to the cabin to get my fishing gear. I had spent an evening before the bear attack working on my fishing equipment, so everything was set up and ready to go.

Down at the water's edge, I leaned my rifle on a log and took a long cast to the center of the river. I hadn't retrieved the lure more than five feet when it was slammed hard, followed by a huge swirl on the surface that boiled the water and sent water droplets far above the surface. The fight was on. Bill and Alvin told me that the river had a healthy pike population, and I hoped this was a pike because both men had agreed that it was a tasty fish. A few minutes later I dragged a ten-pound northern pike onto the sand and rocks. It seemed unbelievable to me that a fish could get so big. Handling it was hard. At this point I was not considered a seasoned fisherman. Hoping my line would not snap or the lure pop out of its mouth, I pulled the fish several yards from the water to a place where I figured it would not be able to flop back into the river. I searched for and found a piece of wood that looked like it would work as a club. I grabbed it and struck him on the head. It worked well. I must have knocked him out cold and broke his neck because he did not move after that.

After the exhilaration of the catch wore off, I realized I did not know how to clean the fish but did have a book on the subject. I would have to take a quick lesson on fish cleaning.

I walked back to the cabin with my fishing rod and the pike in tow and laid the fish on a pile of alder sticks that I had cut earlier in the year. I went inside the cabin to retrieve my book on cleaning fish. There was a general section on how to clean fish, and a section more specific, with a focus on removing the "Y" bones out of a pike fillet. After studying the words and the pictures in the book, I was confident that I could get the fillets off of the carcass by teasing the tip of my knife blade around the rib cage of the fish, thus ending up with two fillets with only one strip of "Y" bones in each.

I grabbed my fillet knife and headed outside to where the fish lay. Just like the book instructed, I cut behind the gills straight down until I felt the blade hit the backbone. Then I made a 45-degree angle and with the tip of my blade about two inches into the fish, the tip just at the top of the rib cage. Guided by the backbone, I cut toward the tail to the point where the last back fin was and about where the ribs ended, then pushed the blade all the way through to the belly side and continued along the back bone until the blade severed the tail end of the fillet from the fish.

That was easy, I thought. The fillet was free and it was beautiful. I was happy with my work. The other side came off with a bit more of a struggle. Besides being a slippery fish, it was generally harder to handle with one slab of the carcass already removed.

Pulling the "Y" bones out of the fish flesh was hard with the skin still attached, so I removed the skin from each fillet in hopes that it would make the process easier. It did help a small bit; however, the aesthetic appeal of the fillet was less pleasing. *Oh well*, I thought, *now I have boneless fish for the fry pan.* My last work with the knife was to cut each fillet into four pieces. They were big chunks of fish, and because I was so hungry, figured I could eat half of the fish for supper.

After carrying my cleaned fish fillets into the cabin, I returned and cleaned up the fish remains. I put the wood used as a cleaning surface in the fire pit and lit the wood on fire. I was just about to throw the carcass in the flames when I saw movement on the side hill where I was digging the hibernation den for Pretty Girl. It was my little bear. She was back. Even though we had not known each other for more than a few days, Pretty Girl came prancing down to the cabin like she owned the place. Her pace down the hillside made it seem like she missed me while she was gone. I know I missed her. She reminded me that I was holding the fish carcass as she pulled it from my hand and devoured it in what seemed like two seconds. *The little gal is hungry,* I thought, and went in the cabin to mix some milk and sugar and leftover grease from frying spam. She greedily consumed this mixture and must have liked it because she continued licking the bowl until I said her name. She looked at me in that quizzical way that said, "What's your problem." I laughed as I started up the hill to finish digging her den, and she followed. I believe that she thought I was her mamma bear. I hoped so. The new role fit me well.

I had accomplished quite a bit that morning and could see that there was not much digging left to do. Before I could continue my work, Pretty Girl commenced to crawl in her den and check it out. She fit quite well, but needed a little more room considering she would pack on a lot of weight before hibernation. I planned on feeding her fish and pancakes with syrup, along with all the milk she could drink. After some gentle prodding with the shovel handle, Pretty Girl scooted out of my way and I continued digging. She was like an overgrown puppy; however, constantly nudging me as she tried to get in the space as I was working it. This, of course made me laugh. I thought about her being a wild animal and how she grew close to me so quickly; the reasoning was simple, I was her mother, her protector. After a short while we were done digging the den and so headed back to the cabin. As time passed I planned to drag some small brush and river grass up the hill so Pretty Girl could line her den and be snuggly warm this winter. As I saw it, she needed all the help she could get to make it through the frigid months without her mother.

Time slipped on by. Before I knew it, we were experiencing much colder weather, with occasional snow falls that covered the ground and did not melt until late afternoon. I spent a lot of time fishing and feeding the fattest parts of the fish to Pretty Girl. In fact, she received all the food she wanted. After a few weeks of this, my little bear was quite rotund and at times looked as if she waddled as she walked. She slept a lot of the time and I found myself walking her to her den where she would spend the majority of the day. Together we had lined the den with grass and other ground fodder; it looked completely comfortable. One night after supper she strolled up to her den as I watched from the cabin door. She turned and looked at me for a long while. After that she entered the den and pulled leaves and branches over the opening. It snowed hard that night. Pretty Girl did not come down for breakfast the next day.

Chapter 22
Trap Preparation

I remembered the next morning very well. It was hard not to see Pretty Girl after we had come to know each other so well in such a short period of time. The snow was deep. Walking outside the cabin was quite difficult at first, but it was only a foot of snow so, I quickly became used to walking in it. I quietly walked up the hill until I was about twenty feet from Pretty Girl's den. It was almost imperceptible under the blanket of pure white. What I did not expect to see but was the indicator that my little bear was alive and breathing, was a small-crystalized hole. It was about the size of a golf ball and was directly on top of the duff she had used to plug the entrance of her den. This was her breathing hole that would supply her with oxygen, the fresh air that would keep her healthy. After that, I figured that if I saw the crystals every time I checked on her, all was well with her.

As the days passed I completed the final work of preparing my traps for the trap line. I also began to think about Bill and Alvin. They could ride their snow machines here without the river being frozen, but it would most likely be that they would wait until complete freeze up. I pulled all the traps from the crates and from the spot where they hung on the outside cabin wall. *There has to be a better way to store these traps after I have them boiled*, I thought. *Maybe I should build a hanger by crossing some heavy willow sticks like an X and wire them together, then pushing the other ends in the snow to hold the whole thing in place. I could lay a ridge pole between the two so that each end of the pole was supported by the crossed sticks. Hmm, good idea.*

I decided that this is what I would do. It took me no time at all to construct my new trap hanger. After that I stoked up the fire and filled my biggest pot with snow until in its melted state, the pot was half full. In the warming water I placed willow bark strips, willow leaves, and spruce needles. These natural smelling ingredients would not only get rid of human scent, they would also dye my traps. I brought this concoction to a boil and then added as many traps as would fit at one time. This process took several days to complete. In my free time, I located the storage tub that held all of my trapping baits and lures and carried it into the cabin. I examined everything to make sure that the needed tools were in their proper places. The rest of my time was spent dreaming of the day when I would set my first trap.

Winter was setting in. The nights were cold, and the river was forming an ever-thickening layer of ice because the days never went above the freezing mark on the thermometer. But, since I still did not have my snow machine, running a trap line was not yet possible. I had to occupy my time with something else. Over time, I found myself quite adept at harvesting ptarmigan with my .22 pistol. That little gun was amazing. One afternoon while I was out looking for a fat ptarmigan to shoot, I saw a beaver swim across a narrow channel that led to a small pond just off the bank of the river. I wondered why that water was open while everything around it was frozen solid. To my untrained eyes this did not look like a beaver set, so I never entertained the idea of placing a trap there until now. It was November 15th and the itch to trap beaver was now unbearable. I made plans to set some beaver traps the next day. Thankfully, this area was close to the cabin and setting some traps without the help of Bill and Alvin, would be good practice for me. On that night I did not find a bird for supper, but did harvest a fat snowshoe hare for my dining pleasure. After cleaning the snowshoe, I set it down in the snow to allow the meat to cool in the late afternoon air. There were several moose across the river. I watched them until I began to shiver. The sight of the moose roused my thinking about moose hunting. *All in good time*, I thought to myself, *all in good time.*

I picked up the now partially frozen hare and was quite amazed at how the temperature had consistently fallen over the last week or so. At this rate, Bill and Alvin would be here soon. Back at the cabin, I cut up the meat into fry pan sizes and rolled them in seasoned flour. I then slow-fried them in vegetable oil. When the meat was just about done cooking, I opened up a can of baked beans, something I had forgotten about in my food storage crates, and put them on the stove to heat up. "Man, what a supper," I said aloud as I licked my fingers clean.

I went to bed as soon as I finished cleaning up the supper dishes. Once again, I found myself missing my little bear friend, but knew she was safe and sound in her den. As I lay down for the night, my mind flooded with images of a big brown beaver lying on white snow. Also, in my fantasy, I saw my cabin filled with drying hides. I do not think I could have held any more excitement in my mind and body without exploding. I lay awake a long time dreaming of the next day.

I know that sleep came because I remembered waking up the following morning. "Snow machines," I whispered aloud, "snow machines!" I jumped out of bed and into my jeans, pulling them up as I hopped to the door just in time to open it and see Bill and Alvin pull up to the cabin.

Chapter 23
Bill and Alvin Help Out

"Hey, good morning. Jeez, am I happy to see you guys!"

"Hello Codi," they chimed in unison. "How has everything been going out here?"

"Excellent," then added, "ah, well, with the exception of a few hiccups."

"Well," Bill said, "that is to be expected. It's not as if a bear attacked you."

"Ha-ha, almost!" I said as I raised my hand with one digit missing.

Both men lost their joviality when they saw my hand.

"What the hell happened, Codi?" Alvin asked.

"I had a confrontation with a bear shortly after you guys left. When it was all said and done, she was dead. I have the runt-cub, Pretty Girl. She is hibernating in a den right up there on the hillside," I said, pointing to the spot while I was talking.

"Oh yeah, and the old sow took my finger off when she charged."

"How did that not get infected?" Bill asked, as he dropped what was in his arms and grabbed my hand to examine it.

"Well, even though I am young, I knew that I had to keep it clean, so I washed it out well and dipped it with iodine several times until it was healed. I kept it wrapped for a few days. That really helped to stop the bleeding."

"Do you feel any pain now?" asked Alvin.

"No," I said, "at least not constant pain. If I bump it on something it hurts for a bit."

"You are lucky to be alive," Bill replied, with an astonished look on his face.

"I know," I replied." I have learned a lot since that day."

"And what is it you have learned?" asked Alvin.

"The most important thing is to be aware of my surroundings and to respect everything around me."

"Well, those are good lessons," Bill said. "But the loss of a finger is a heck of a price to pay."

"I can assure you guys that it will not happen again."

"Let's hope not," Bill said as he picked up the items he had dropped.

As we talked about the bear attack and many other things that transpired since I last saw my friends, my eyes continually traveled to my new snow machine, which rested on a sled behind Bill's machine. The bear story was old news to me. That snow machine was now my top priority.

"Can we unload my machine?" I asked, interrupting the present conversation.

"You bet, Codi. Release the tension on the tie downs and the cinch straps. Your new machine is full of gas, and we brought fifty gallons in the barrel on the sled behind Alvin's machine."

"Thanks, guys, this is awesome!"

"We also chipped in and bought a turkey and a couple bags of potatoes and carrots."

"Wow! Incredible! We will have a fine thanksgiving dinner."

I was so happy to see my friends. I realized it had been about three months since I had talked to another person. The only other words spoken were to Pretty Girl, and occasionally, to myself.

I stared at my new machine and mumbled to myself, "She is a beauty. Will you teach me to ride today?"

"Yes, we will," said Bill. "And if you will have us, we would like to stay for a few days."

"Absolutely!" I said, my smile beaming widely across my face.

Alvin broke in and said, "After we do some things here we want to ride out to the head of my trap line and make a trail that connects to Bill's area."

"Does this mean that we will see each other during the trapping season?"

"Yes, occasionally, is our hope" Bill said. "We would like to use your cabin as a sleep over spot once in a while if everything goes as planned, but everything depends on the weather. Staying with you will reduce the amount of back tracking we have to do.

"That is fine with me!"

"Well, alright then, we have a plan."

Besides the potatoes and carrots my friends brought eggs, bacon, butter, and bread. These things were a real treat. I missed having eggs and bacon on a regular basis. We all agreed that we were hungry, so into the cabin we went and cooked up a huge breakfast of eggs, bacon, potatoes, and pancakes. I opened a jar of blueberries and made syrup for the pancakes.

Bill and Alvin seemed to be impressed with my progress. And, as I thought about it, realized that so much had happened since I last saw my friends. We talked about everything on the planet. They gave me news about what was going on in the big old world, and happily none of it concerned me. Out here I did not have to put up with bickering politicians, and squabbling people on the so-called reality shows that they told me about. None of that mattered to me, and I found that I was very happy with my place in the wild. As we continued our conversation I told my friends of the place where I was ready to set beaver traps. Both men were excited, and immediately saw this as an easy opportunity to teach me some trapping skills.

After breakfast, and breakfast clean up, we finished prepping the snow machine and then took a couple of short rides around the cabin so I could get used to this big and powerful machine. I could not believe how much power was under the hood, and at how huge the machines looked parked in the snow. I put the maintenance manual in the cabin so I could continue reading it after dark. I did not think driving the snow machine was that hard as long as I remembered to lean and use my weight to control its balance and its direction. Ultimately, I found that riding with one knee on the seat gave me the best results for controlling the rig. The other foot was on the running board, which effectively made me stand while riding. After the practice runs, we unloaded the fuel barrel and other goodies from Alvin's sled. We then loaded the axe, traps, dried alder poles, and some other odds and ends into one of the sleds. For added practice, we each drove our own machine to the spot where I would begin my beaver-trapping career.

"This is a good spot," remarked Alvin, as we stopped in front of the spot I was at the day before.

"See how the channel narrows as it comes off the river and leads to this small pond. Every beaver in the area will swim that channel. This is one of the easiest sets to make. Now, grab two of those alder poles and let's get started."

I grabbed them and asked, "We need wire, correct?"

"Yes, we do."

Bill took the two dried alder poles, crossed them about a foot from the top, and then wired them tightly together at that point.

"You see," he said, "like a two-legged teepee, they can't be pulled apart once the bottom ends are set in the channel. And, since we have about four inches of ice already in this channel and it will be cold tonight, your set will freeze in and be securely anchored."

After this demonstration, I asked, "Then the 330-Conibear will be set and be anchored to the bottom of the two poles, and be underwater, correct?"

"Exactly, young man," said Bill in a complementary tone. "Grab those setting tongs and a trap and I will show you how it is done."

After he had everything situated, Bill expertly used the tongs to easily set the trap.

"Be sure to keep all body parts away from the trap while you are setting it," he explained, "and when you handle it after it is set, be extremely careful; if it springs, anything in its jaws will be crushed."

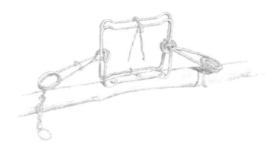

I paid close attention to Bill's words. It was clear to me that any animal caught in this trap would be killed instantly. Since I never wanted anything to suffer, I liked the concept of the 330-Conibear trap. Together, Bill and I wired the trap in place while Alvin chopped a neat hole in the ice that would accommodate the entire set. The hole ended up being about twenty inches long and six inches wide. It ran perpendicular to the channel so a beaver was forced to swim through the set trap and be caught. The hole in the ice was more than enough area to get the trap and poles through and securely anchored in the mud at the bottom of the channel.

"You see," said Bill, "why I left the three inches of alder pole below where the bottom of the trap is wired?"

"Yes, I see, so it anchors in the mud and cannot be pulled free."

"Correct, after this freezes up a bit, the set will not move."

"Sweet," was my only response.

"Then," Bill said, "As an added precaution, we wire the trap chain to another alder branch which we simply leave lying on top of the ice. This way you will never lose a trap."

"This set is done," I said with incredible excitement piping in my voice. "Let's do another!"

I picked up my tools and put them back in the sled. After a short ride around the pond, we identified two more places to make sets. After these sets were constructed in the same manner as the first, we scanned the area and admired our work. All three of us stood there smiling like the mouse that got the last piece of cheese without getting caught in the mousetrap. The sets looked great. I could tell that both of my dear friends were reliving their youths, and, most likely, it was because I was a willing learner, and that they had someone in their lives to share their knowledge with. At this point in our relationship and so many times after this one, I was extremely thankful that Bill and Alvin had come into my life, and, I knew, that they were thankful that I was in their lives. With anticipation for the next morning, we headed back to the cabin for a well-deserved supper and a good night's sleep.

Chapter 24
Beaver!

Early the next morning we found ourselves sitting around the wood stove sipping hot coffee and devouring piles of pancakes and bacon and eggs for breakfast. I peeked outside and saw that snow was falling. Alvin had checked the forecast before they left Fairbanks, and knew that it would not add up to more than a couple of inches. The gently falling snow was a beautiful sight, but was second in line to my excitement about checking the traps, Bill and Alvin shared my enthusiasm. We took our time; however, and enjoyed the morning. After we had enough coffee and talk, we decided to get on with the day.

"Well, let's go boys," Bill said.

"Yes", Alvin answered. "If we have beaver in the traps, there will be a lot of work ahead of us, and if the pelts look good, we should set more traps along the river before dark sets in."

"I agree," said Bill. "We must take advantage of the daylight and this time of year when the snow is not very deep and trap the places close to home."

"Also, this will give me some skinning, fleshing, and stretching practice of pelts while you guys are still here to help me," I said, hoping for their agreement.

"Well, Bill is by far the better skinner between the two of us, but I sure can stretch a beaver hide so we get the maximum price," said Alvin.

"The bigger the hide, the better the money?" I asked.

"Yes, basically speaking," said Alvin, "but you never stretch them too thin. The fur buyer knows this trick and will not give you a good price because he can feel and see the paper thinness of the hide. The buyer needs fur that is thick and luscious for the high-end garment market."

"Thanks, that is good to know. I want to learn how to do it correctly," I said.

Outside, we started our machines and let them warm up while we checked the sleds for all needed materials. As soon as we were satisfied that we had everything, we hit the trail leading to the pond. The trail was easily visible since not much snow had fallen; it was nice that we were going over it again, so it would become packed and well defined with each trip. In single file order, we approached and stopped in front of the first set; a place that I was sure held a beaver in the 330-Conibear. It did. After brushing away the freshly fallen snow, I could see through the clear ice that the trap was sprung, and there just below the ice was a gigantic beaver tail floating in the water.

"Beaver!" I yelled like a small child who is unwrapping gifts on Christmas morning. "It's a big one!"

Bill and Alvin came to my side, both men smiling. "Yes, that is a beauty," Bill exclaimed along with Alvin's, "Oh, yes, a very nice beaver."

I grabbed my ice spud and began chopping around the hole that Alvin had cut the night before.

"Be careful," Alvin reminded me as he grabbed the chisel to slow my process. "If you chop too deep you will hit the beaver and cut the hide and that means damaged fur and lost profit."

"I will be careful!" I huffed, as I lightened the weight of my strokes on the ice.

"Make the hole much bigger," Bill suggested. "You have to pull that big critter through it."

I did as I was instructed and in no time was hefting a super-size male beaver onto the ice. I laid him in the snow and just stood there gazing at my catch.

"My first catch as a trapper," I said with unparalleled exuberance. "I am so freaking excited I could jump to the moon."

"Excellent work, Codi, this is a special time in every trapper's life. It is something you will never forget, but it is also where the real work of a trapper begins. This catch creates a whole bunch of work for you. You must always properly care for anything you take from nature and that means skinning and stretching all of your catches."

"That I will do. I promise."

"Okay, Codi, let's get that trap off of the beaver so that beautiful hide does not freeze to the metal," said Bill.

"Will do!" I replied as I grabbed the setting tongs in one hand, and then knelt on the ice and placed the notched end of the tongs in the spring eyes of the trap and squeezed them together. After I heard the automatic lock on the tongs click, locking everything in place, I released my grip and put the safety lock on the 330-Conibear to the locked position, then did the same for the other side. I pulled the trap off the beaver, dropped it on the ground, and then grabbed both hind legs of the huge animal. I had all I could do to heft his entire body off the ground.

"What a beast!" I grunted from my strained position. "I did not think beaver grew this big."

"They get even bigger than this, Codi."

"You are kidding, right, Bill?"

"No, this one will weigh in at about fifty or sixty pounds. I have caught beaver well over seventy pounds."

"Wow!" was all I could muster in response.

Alvin began remaking the set, which is not something I had considered. In my novice mind, I thought we were done in this spot. Remaking the set made perfect sense as there should be great numbers of beaver coming through this channel. I jumped in to help Alvin with the set. My anticipation was high for another catch down the line.

After the trap was back in place, we loaded up the tools and the first catch of the day and moved to the second set which held a smaller beaver, but still quite large in my eyes. I figured she would weigh in at thirty pounds. The third set was empty. We did not touch the third set because Alvin and Bill believed it would produce a beaver in the next few days. All in all, this was a great morning for the three of us.

Before heading back to the cabin, we followed the river downstream and found the beaver activity to be extremely high. Bill and Alvin figured I could take ten to fifteen beaver out of that couple of miles of river without worry of over trapping. They advised me many times to not trap out any area. "If you do," they always said, "you will have nothing to trap next year." That made perfect sense to me.

After completing our scouting journey, we made six more sets along the river and the adjoining ponds and sloughs. We could walk on the ice in these shallow ponds because there was little or no current and the wind never churned the water up enough to keep it from freezing. Still, we had to be extremely careful when on top of a beaver channel because of the beaver activity directly under the ice would keep it thin. The movement from the beaver swimming in the channel disrupts the stillness of the water and therefore the ice does not freeze as thick as other parts of the pond. I found this out the hard way when I stepped where I should not have placed my foot.

Just as I heard Bill yell, "Not there, Codi!" I felt the thin ice break beneath my left foot. I went all the way to my crotch with one leg in the frigid water and the other splayed out on top of the ice so I looked like a slingshot with its handle missing.

"Oh, that is cold!" I screamed as I rolled out of the water.

"Are you okay?" my friends questioned repeatedly with alarmed smiles on their faces.

"Yes! I think so. Dang! That water is cold."

"Ha-ha," was Bill's response. "You are lucky in two ways; one, the water is shallow and, two, we are here. Be cautious with every step you take in this country. You get very few second chances."

"Yes, I am beginning to see that." After hearing Bill's words, I recalled the bear incident from a few months ago and how that incident could have ended much worse than it did.

"Well, Bill said, with a big grin still on his face, "since you made a hole there, and we know there is a channel below it, let's make this set number ten."

Even though I was wet and cold, and a bit ornery, I agreed to make the set and then call it a day as far as beaver trapping was concerned. After we got back to the cabin I changed into a dry set of clothes and then we enjoyed a hot meal. I, as well as my friends felt good about the morning. The first two beavers of the year lay near the stove, their hides drying in the warm cabin air.

Chapter 25
Meat for the Table

After we were done eating, Bill and Alvin said they would help me skin the first beaver. After that they wanted to head out and do some scouting on their lines while I skinned the second beaver. The men said they would be back in a few hours, but surely after dark, to instruct me on how to flesh the hides and then stretch them.

As I quickly learned, skinning a beaver is hard work. We worked hard together on the first one. Bill and Alvin had many pointers to give. After each lesson they taught me, I was handed the knife and had to practice what I learned, so it took a long time to get the first hide off the carcass. One very important pointer they gave was to skin the beaver so that the fat stayed on the body, not on the hide. Bill reiterated what Alvin showed me by saying, "It is double the work if you leave the fat on the hide, making the fleshing that much tougher to do."

We were almost done, but the lessons continued. "The hardest part is skinning around the ears, the eyes, the nose, and the mouth," Bill said. "To get the best price from the fur dealer, a trapper's hides must look their best."

"Okay, Codi, the other one is yours," were Bill's final words for the time being.

"Thanks guys," I said with some lack of confidence in my voice.

My two friends washed their hands and exited the cabin to start their snow machines as I began skinning the second beaver. Before leaving, Alvin told me to save the beaver meat, and he would use it to make a pot of chili. He said the meat makes the best chili because it is rich in flavor. When I finished skinning the beaver, I took the carcass outside were we had placed the other one and cut off all four legs of each, then disconnected the ribs from the backbone and saved the backbone from head to tail. There was a lot of meat on these pieces, and after we ground it up with the hand meat grinder, according to Alvin, we would have the perfect chili meat.

I did not want to flesh the hides without Bill and Alvin, so to make good use of my time I deboned all the meat and set up my grinder and ran the meat through. It worked perfectly. I saved all the bones, fat, and innards as bait for trapping lynx, fox, wolves, and wolverines. I laid them in small piles in the snow so they would freeze solidly. After that I would put them in a tub for storage until I needed the bait. Making separate chunks of bait would benefit me because I would not have to spend so much time chopping bait off a big hunk of frozen meat while out on the trap line.

It was getting late. The sky was unusually dark, and I thought it might snow, or, for some reason, I thought it might warm up and rain. It passed without any precipitation. I felt better because I figured any precipitation would complicate the next day of hunting and checking traps. After thinking about the weather a bit more, I figured it would make no difference to Bill and Alvin, and therefore should make no difference to me. It was part of life out here. Besides that, they had probably encountered every situation known to man, and could easily handle themselves. That is what I hoped for, at least.

It was 10pm before my waiting ears recognized the faint sound of snow machines approaching the cabin. It was Bill and Alvin. Finally, they were back from their excursion. Outside the cabin, I could hear their excited discussion as they gathered what was needed to be brought in from the sleds. As they entered the cabin, I noticed that each man wore a smile on his face. They had found prime sign in their trapping territories or something just as good.

"Did you guys find what you were looking for?" I asked.

"We did!" they chimed, "and much more!"

"What is the more?" I questioned, as their excitement enhanced mine.

"Well, just now, as we were coming up the river, we spotted a nice cow moose with no calves. She will likely still be close by tomorrow morning."

"Should we go get her?"

"Yes, in the morning," Bill replied.

"We all need meat," said Alvin. "With no calf, and being an older animal, she is a good choice for us."

"She will supply plenty of meat," said Bill, to both of us. "The first priority of the morning is to harvest that moose."

"Okay," I said. "Let's make plans over supper."

I had assembled a pan full of scrambled eggs that had everything in them but the kitchen sink. We had accumulated some leftovers from previous meals and they needed to be used. There was leftover spam that was originally meant for sandwiches, some onion tidbits, bacon, and a chunk of cheese that I diced into small pieces. I stirred it all together, and when I had first heard the snow machines coming, put it on top of the wood stove to cook. We had plenty of bread and butter, so just before the eggs were done cooking, I threw six pieces of bread on the stovetop to toast. After a couple minutes they were buttered and we were eating. Bill and Alvin were hungry; we all shoveled in mouthfuls of food before we started a conversation.

158

The eating pace slowed and Bill said, "I think we should drive until we see her, then stop the machines at a place where Codi can make a good, clean shot."

"Me!" I exclaimed in a somewhat panicked tone.

"Yes, you. You have been practicing, and your rifle is sighted in, correct?"

"Yes, Bill, to both questions, but what if I miss?" I asked, still worried.

"Bill and I will be on your flanks, if it looks like she is going to run off after you shoot, we will take a shot to finish her."

"Okay, that sounds good to me." At first, I envisioned just me and the moose in a showdown. I felt better.

After our conversation, and knowing that Bill and Alvin would back me up, I still felt some apprehension about being selected as the one who would kill the moose. It was not because I did not want to kill her, after all, I had dreamt of this moment for a long time, rather, I was worried that I would miss, and all of Bill and Alvin's hard work would be for nothing. I knew I had to do it, and also knew that my friends had years of experience with this type of thing. Finally, I found my confidence, and that is what gave me some peace of mind.

The conversation dwindled as we finished supper. Quickly thereafter we were off to bed. I could not sleep for what seemed like an eternity. My mind raced with the thought of a giant moose hitting the ground, and me standing over it. My thoughts were all good because I knew that this moose was going to feed at least three families. Part of our discussion during supper was about how to divide up the meat.

I thought that one quarter would be enough for me; that way Bill and Alvin would have the majority to take back with them. Some of the meat would be shared with Alvin's nephews. Alvin told me while trapping that it would be likely that I would encounter some caribou during the winter, and that they are excellent table fare. That excited me. After all, I had enough jars for preserving meat if I did get a caribou, and, of course, could keep chunks frozen outside the cabin during the winter months. If a caribou did not grace my rifle sights, there were plenty of ptarmigan, hare, and fish for me to catch and eat, and I was quite adept at putting them in the fry pan. Finally sleep came as my last thoughts of the day entered the dream world and I dreamed of the next day's activities.

Bill was up first; he made coffee, which was an unwritten requirement that the early riser, I learned, was obligated to perform. The noise in the cabin was pleasing, and the smells were even better. By the time I sat up in my bunk I knew there were pancakes in the fry pan. I pulled on my long johns, jeans, and boots and threw a jacket over my shoulders and headed out to my makeshift outhouse to take care of my morning business. The air was much warmer than the previous few mornings. Even though it was still dark, I could feel that the daylight hours would be unseasonably warm and maybe wet. I thought about the dark clouds the day before and figured maybe they were coming back to soak us in rain. As I trotted back to the cabin, I noticed the beaver hides. Just for good measure, before going back inside, I shoveled a pile of snow over them. We would have to stretch them soon, but for now I did not want the hides to get pecked at from birds and needed them to stay as cold as possible until I could tend to them.

After I finished covering the hides, I leaned the shovel against the outside wall and entered the cabin, I saw Bill and Alvin eating pancakes and drinking their coffee. I poured myself a cup and sat down to tell them about the weather.

I said, "It is much warmer today than yesterday."

"I know," said Alvin.

"How do you know? You have not been outside yet."

"You are correct, but as Bill was firing up the stove, I noticed that there were a few coals remaining in the bottom of the fire box and that the cabin was still cozy warm."

"Oh, that makes sense. If it is warmer outside of the cabin, it will be warmer inside the cabin even if there is very little heat coming from the stove."

Our conversation quickly changed from the temperature to moose hunting. I asked the men if they thought the moose was still in the same spot.

"Well, probably not in the same spot, but close by," Bill said.

"How far of a ride is it?"

"Oh, it must be six to eight miles out," said Alvin.

With that, Bill scanned our plates to make sure all were done eating and then finalized the conversation. "Let's pack up everything we need. Make sure your knives are sharp." And then added, "Alvin, do you have the bone saw?"

"Yes sir, I do."

"Excellent!"

"Let's hit the trail."

Light was just beginning to color the sky as we stepped outside to start our machines. Bill instructed me that when we found the moose and were at a good spot for me to take the shot, he and Alvin would come to a stop side by side. He went on to say that they would be about ten feet apart, and that I was expected to park even with them, but in between them, thus forming the flanking situation he spoke of last night.

He asked if I understood. I said that I did.

On the ride out, I could not help to reflect on my life to this point. *Here I am at the ripe old age of eighteen, living a life that I felt was meant for me. I wondered what my old friends were doing. Do they think about me?* I knew for sure that my old life was something I would never return to. Even at this young age, with all that had happened since my parents had passed away, I knew I was going in the right direction. Out here I thought: *This is the only place where a person can learn the meaning of life, not just the wilds of Alaska, but the wilds of anywhere. As long as a person has seclusion, he can figure out why he is on earth.* I was learning a lot; these past five or six months had taught me more about life than the first seventeen and a half years of my life. Meeting Bill and Alvin was something I did not plan for, but was so happy that it happened, and grateful that they were my friends.

I was deep in thought and went right past Bill and Alvin before they gently gunned their engines and pulled up alongside of me, frowns on their faces.

"Hey," Bill said in a hushed tone. "We are close and it is light enough to see and shoot."

"Okay, Bill, I am ready," I said as I removed my rifle that was strapped across my shoulder and set it on my lap.

"Here is the plan," said Alvin. "We will crest this hill and stop just like we discussed when we made our plan back at the cabin. If she is not there, we will scan the area and then move on to check over the next hill."

"Okay," I whispered.

"Ready, Bill?"

"Yes, Alvin, let's go."

We softly moved forward in the heavy, wet snow. My excitement and anticipation increased as we motored slowly up the hill and came to a stop. There she stood, like a magical illusion, as if she were waiting for us. I could tell that she was an old moose, and that, like Bill said yesterday, would be a good animal to harvest. I shouldered my gun as Bill whispered to me, "Not yet, let her get completely broadside to us."

"Okay," I shakily whispered. "Tell me when."

It seemed like forever that she stood and looked at us, her with big black eyes and me with the shouldered rifle peering through it, ready to fire. I did not sense any fear in her, and was happy for that. Finally, she must have deemed that we were not a considerable threat and took a few steps and turned broadside.

With a mixture of excitement and his heavy breathing, Bill whispered in a gravely tone. "Now!"

From my steady stance leaning on the sturdy snow machine windshield, I calmed my nerves and put the crosshairs of the scope on her vital organs and pulled the trigger. I saw the bullet's impact through the scope and watched her jump as high in the air as a big moose could, and kick her hind legs even higher. She took off running.

"Don't shoot again. It's over," Alvin whispered hoarsely.

"She will go down," Bill said, with his rifle still slung over his shoulder, apparently confident with my shot.

"She went down! I saw her! I saw her! She is down! She is just beyond that clump of willows," I excitedly shouted into the wind that was now spitting sleet in our faces.

"Nice shot, young man, Bill replied to my excitement. "She didn't know what hit her; that is the way it should be."

The words of my two mentors rang clearly in my mind as I stood alongside them gazing at the dead moose lying seventy-five yards away. As I think back on this time, I realized that this was a pinnacle in my lifetime. It was the first moment that I fully realized that I could live off the land. Also, I vowed that from that day forward, I would not spend any more of my inherited money unless it was absolutely necessary. "No," I said aloud, "I will live off the land as much as possible." My friends just stood there grinning at me. They knew what I was experiencing and let it play out to the fullest.

After a moment to calm our nerves, we jumped on our snow machines and slowly approached the moose. Alvin took the lead, and after determining that she was dead, pulled his sled so close to her that I saw the hair move on the moose's back. I later learned that this was important because of the size of the animal and the depth of the snow. Snow depth can make gutting and cutting up of a moose extra hard work. With the snow machine and sled close to the animal the amount of movements a hunter has to make are reduced. An animal this big cannot be dragged; it must be placed on the sled for transport. Because of the amount of work that had to be done, we decided that we should gut her out and do the cut-up work back at the cabin. This was a good idea since there were ten beaver traps to check, and at least two beaver to flesh and stretch.

As I quickly learned, there is a definite technique to loading such a large animal onto a sled. After we completed the gutting job, we wedged the long side of the sled as far as possible under the moose following the spine from the base of the neck all the way to the rump. Once the sled was wedged in place, Alvin stood behind it with his feet and legs holding the sled so that it would not slide out of position. With his two free hands, Alvin put considerable downward pressure on the other long side of the sled. Bill and I grabbed the legs from the belly side of the moose and swung them over toward Alvin, and just like that she rolled over onto the sled. Alvin quickly moved away from the sled as it flattened out on the snow with the moose cradled snuggly in, held perfectly in place by the sides of the sled. We then tied ropes around her hooves and tied all of the legs together so the moose was a tightly bound package on the sled. After a tarp was thrown over the big moose, and a couple of tie-down straps fastened over her, she was secured in place. We headed for home with gratitude in our hearts for the fine morning of hunting.

The ride home was slow, but we made it without any problems. We stopped the machines in front of the cabin and then untied the moose and rolled her off the sled. We positioned her so she was lying on her stomach, her legs splayed out in an effort to keep her balanced in that position. Bill said he was going to chop five spruce poles to make a hanging rack for the meat. After explaining his plan, Bill departed upstream while Alvin and I began skinning the moose.

"You see," Alvin said, "take your knife and insert it under the skin just at the base of the skull and zip all the way along the spine to the base of the tail."

With one quick and seemingly effortless motion he made this long cut.

"Do I start from this side and skin down toward the belly?" I asked from where I stood on the other side of the dead animal.

"Yep, Codi, that is what you do, and I do the same on this side."

I began to skin my side of the moose. We worked diligently across from each other until each of us finished skinning as far as we could. Together we rolled the moose to one side so the skinned-out meat sat on top of its own hide. From there Alvin showed me how to skin the legs so that we could keep the hide in one piece.

As we worked, Alvin offered, "I will take that bear skin and this moose skin and have them tanned for you if that is to your liking."

"It is to my liking. Excellent!" I said in a thankful tone.

"They will serve you well in many ways," Alvin explained. "Carry them with you always in the winter as part of your survival gear. They could save your life someday."

"I will," I promised.

Our work was progressing rapidly, and after a few more minutes we were almost done skinning. Bill returned with the four-inch diameter spruce logs strapped in his sled. We unloaded them and quickly assembled a hanging rack. It was not extremely cold out, but cold enough to properly cool the meat. Back at the moose carcass Bill detached the front and hindquarter from the top half of the moose and with considerable effort from the three of us, we got them hung on the meat pole. Bill and I each grabbed a leg on the bottom half of the carcass and rolled her over and detached the last two quarters of meat. We hung them beside the other two, and then hoisted, and hung the rib cage and neck. We stood back and admired our work. It had been a long day, but the rewards made it all worthwhile.

"It is getting late in the day," said Bill. "Why don't you and Alvin go check the beaver traps and I will stay here and finish up. We will have fried heart sandwiches for supper."

"Sounds like a plan," I said.

Alvin and I jumped on our machines and headed for the first of the nine sets. Again, the first trap held a nice beaver. It was not as big as the one yesterday, but still a nice size beaver. "Number three!" I exclaimed at the top of my lungs. I chopped through the ice and pulled the beaver and trap through the hole, freed the beaver from the trap, and, as Alvin instructed, put the trap in his sled.

"We should not remake this set until we see how many more beavers we catch. Remember, we have to leave seed for next year."

"Oh, I see, that is a good idea," I said as I looked ahead toward the next set.

The next two sets were empty, and a sense of disappointment set in me. My excitement was quickly regenerated; however, because the last six sets held three more beaver and one land otter. That added up to six beaver and one otter for a two-day total.

"What a catch," I said to Alvin.

"Yes", he said, "it is. Now let's go back and pickup all the sets we let lay on top of the ice. I think we have enough work to do before Bill and I have to make the trek home."

"Sounds good to me. This sure is a nice start to the season, isn't it, Alvin?"

"Yes, it is, and now that all of your sets are pulled, you are ready to concentrate on land animals. They are prime now, and while you trap them, keep your eyes peeled for fresh places to make beaver sets."

"I will. You can be sure of that."

We turned our machines around and finished picking up our traps and gear as we headed back to the cabin. Just as promised, Bill had finished all the work and had moose heart frying in the pan next to baked beans bubbling in a steaming pot. That supper was the best I had ever eaten.

Since there was so much work ahead of us and it would be a long night if we intended to finish everything, we got to work right after supper. Bill skinned all the beaver, Alvin fleshed them, and I stretched them. It was a great experience and I learned a lot about how to properly care for my hides. Before I went to bed I sat in the dim lamplight and enjoyed the symphony of my friend's cabin shaking snores. Too, I was reliving the beauty of the day's harvest. Finally, my eyelids were too heavy to hold open, and my pleasant thoughts had to be put on hold. I lay down and closed my eyes to a welcome and peaceful sleep.

Chapter 26
Goodbye for Now--My Friends

After breakfast the next morning we placed all of the meat in some game bags that Bill and Alvin brought with them. These would keep the meat clean on the trip back home. I kept the equivalent of one hindquarter of the moose. I decided to spend the rest of the day canning all of the rough cuts, and since the weather had turned much colder overnight, would cut up ten or fifteen pounds for steaks and roasts and freeze them outside. After we had everything packed up for my two friends, we discussed their return to my camp. They said it would be after Christmas, and maybe as late as the New Year.

Wow, I thought, *that sounds odd. Christmas. New Year. These celebrations had not been on my mind for a long time.*

I had been out of modern society long enough to forget about all the things that used to dominate my life. That life felt extremely foreign to me, and for that, I was happy.

"During our absence, you will be trapping full force, correct?"

"Yes sir, Bill, I plan on setting my marten line tomorrow."

"Excellent," said Bill as each man nodded in a satisfied manner.

"We will set our lines on the way into town and check them daily as a team. We decided to work this way because, at our ages, running a trap line is too much for one man."

"That puts my mind to rest," I said, "I was worried about both of you being out there alone."

"Us too, us too."

"Would you guys do me a favor?"

"Name it."

"I need supplies, and have a list and money here for you."

"Sure, we will bring it when we see you after Christmas."

"Thanks, guys, and if there is anything else you think of, or you guys need, buy it out of this bundle of five thousand dollars."

"We are not buying anything for ourselves with your money," Bill said.

"That is for sure!" said Alvin.

"Well, just in case, you know you can use some."

"Thanks, Codi," the men chimed.

"What we will do is bring more gas. Be careful with what you have."

"I will."

With that, my dear friends hopped on their machines and were gone. I was back on my own. There was so much to be done, so I wasted no time cutting and canning the meat, especially because I wanted to get an early start tomorrow morning, the first morning of my solo-trapping career.

Chapter 27
The Unexpected

Well before sun rise I was up and packing my supplies for the first day on my marten trap line. The line was less than five miles long, but would offer me plenty of trapping opportunities. I loaded a full array of traps and supplies into the sled. I did this by using a couple of the metal tubs that I had bought, strapping them in place at the front of the sled. Behind them, I put my waterproof emergency pack that held all my life saving essentials. I did not pack food other than a heart sandwich that I tucked in the breast pocket of my parka. All my lures and baits were in a separate pack that was strapped to my back. I was ready.

The early winter daylight was breaking as I stopped my machine at the head of the trail. I had seen marten sign here earlier in the year so figured it would be the perfect spot to begin my trap line. From all the reading and studying of diagramed trap sets, I felt totally confident in my abilities. At my first set, I walked up to a spruce and chopped the branches off the tree from the ground up to about the top of my head in height. I did this all around the tree. When I got to the highest row of branches on the back and sides of the tree, I only chopped half way through the branches and let them dangle down the trunk. I did this because I wanted to force the marten to come up the front side of the tree. I then nailed a #1½ Victor long spring to the tree just under the remaining branches. These branches served as a ceiling to the set. I set the trap with the dog (The dog holds the jaws down by latching under the pan) toward the top of the tree. A few inches above that I nailed a piece of beaver tail and then squirted a tiny bit of marten urine at the base of the tree.

After I nailed the chain to the backside of the tree, the set was complete. I thought to myself, *It looks good, and now,* I continued in my thought, *I need to make twenty more sets like this one before nightfall.*

I certainly did a lot of thinking and talking to myself these days. Almost none of it was out loud. I had always been a quiet person, so such conversation suited me just fine.

I traversed my trail setting traps wherever sign looked good as long as it was far enough away from the last set. There was no reason crowding sets together. All in all I made eighteen marten sets between the start of my trail to where it came out to the river where I had shot the bear earlier in the year. As soon as I arrived at that spot, I noticed that there was a heavy trail in the snow leading to where I had buried the sow bear. There appeared to be a number of different animals going in and digging in the grave. Some of the tracks I knew were wolves; I could hear them howling from this direction almost every night. I quickly focused my mind on what I had read about snaring wolves, and since I had snares, decided to place one each at two different trails that led to the bear's gravesite. One was set where the wolves' trail went between two spruce saplings. With as little disturbance to the surroundings as possible, I hung the snare from the top of the taller of the two trees and then securely wired it to a big spruce immediately to the left. I made sure the snare was properly supported and at the proper height with a guide wire to hold it in place. It seemed like a good set to my amateur eyes. Tomorrow, I hoped, would tell the truth and there would be a dead wolf in the snare. The other set was in a brushy area just a little further out; it was about thirty feet from the grave. The brush alongside the trail helped secure the snare in place. This set, when finished, was wired to a freshly fallen spruce pole that was still green and about twenty feet long.

No wolf will pull that, I figured.

I stepped back and admired my handiwork, then brushed my boot tracks out as I backed away from the set area.

Twenty sets out today! I kept repeating in my mind. *Twenty sets out today! What will tomorrow offer?*

I jumped on my snow machine and headed for the cabin. It was only then that I realized that I had not taken time to eat my lunch.

Oh heck, I thought. *It will be my lunch tomorrow.*

With that thought, I punched the gas and zoomed home along the frozen river's edge!

I passed the night away by reading trapping stories and watching the clock as if it would magically be morning the next time I looked at it. I tried to be tired, but sleep would not come, even after I lay down in my bed. My excitement was too high for my mind to rest. Eventually, as I lay there, my mind wandered to other things and I realized that I had used up a pretty good chunk of my wood pile, and would have to dedicate time tomorrow to cut some trees and get them hauled back to the cabin to be bucked up and split. I figured my time on the trap line the next day would not be an all-day adventure, leaving me time for this essential work. The thought of cutting wood must have worked to put me to sleep because the next thing I remember was opening my eyes in the complete darkness and hearing the wind howling outside my cabin. From my bed, I grabbed one of my dad's old zippo lighters, flipped open the lid, and struck the flint. The light shone on the clock at my bedside. It was eight o'clock in the morning. *Dang*, I thought, *what the heck is up with that wind?*

I rose from my bed and lit the lantern at my bedside and then made my way to the door and opened it. "A blizzard," I said aloud. "This changes my plans."

I closed the door and went to stoke up the fire. I did not have much dry wood in the cabin so decided that as soon as it got light outside, I would trek to my wood pile and carry in as much as I could stack along the wall by the stove. I made a pot of coffee and sat by the window watching as light slowly crept over the horizon. It was nine thirty before I could see well enough to venture outside. The snow was coming down heavily as the wind whipped in all directions around the cabin. Something told me that this would be a waiting game. I donned my heavy winter garb and my Muck boots that went up to the knees and then plunged head first into the cold wind and tramped a trail to the woodpile.

Because of the wind, there was not a huge amount of snow on the wood, but it was drifted all around the pile and the cabin. I grabbed an armful and trekked back inside. I repeated this until I figured I had enough wood to last for five or six days. It took up a lot of space in the cabin, but it was necessary to have an ample supply of dry wood for the stove. After this job was completed, I went back outside to fire up my snow machine and then back in the cabin where I sat down and drank the rest of my coffee and ate the moose heart sandwich I had saved from the day before. I became restless as I thought about my desire to get out and check my traps. After some consideration, and with Bill and Alvin's advice about being careful ringing in my ears, I decided that because my trail was well defined and mostly in a wooded area, that I would be fine. I dressed for the weather and prepared to hit the trail.

The snow machine was warm, so I shut it off and unloaded most of what was in my sled. If the weather cooperated, I would make it through my trail and have a bunch of dried spruce logs and some fur when I got back to the cabin. I filled my chainsaw with gas and oil, but left the gas can and oil can behind since I would only be cutting the trees in eight-foot sections, and would do some limb work if necessary. I did not take extra traps, but did strap in my survival pack and an extra pack to keep any fur that I caught clean and dry. Finally, I was ready. I pointed the snow machine toward the river, and through the wind and snow, went upriver until I hit the trailhead and my first set.

I hoped the traps would be full on this, my first day. I knew that was unlikely, but had read many trapping and hunting articles that strongly suggested that animals move heavily for feeding purposes just before a big storm hits.

The first trap was untouched. Everything seemed normal, and there was no new sign on top of the snow. I did not get off the machine, and after a short scan of the area, put the machine in motion toward the second set.

"Nothing!" I said aloud, "Dang it!"

My heart sank in disappointment, as it seemed all my dreams for a big catch were disappearing.

Oh well, I have many more sets to check, I thought to myself.

As I approached the third set, something seemed to be out of order. At first, I could not figure it out, but as I got closer I could see the difference.

"Marten! A big male marten! My first marten!" I must have repeated myself a hundred times as I stood there in a trance trying to decide if what I was seeing was what I was actually seeing. Finally, reality struck me and there before me was the first marten I had ever caught. He was beautiful, and the set had worked perfectly. It was a front foot catch, and he was dead with little sign of struggle. I squeezed the trap spring, releasing the jaws which held him. My big marten tumbled to the ground at my feet. I reset the trap and hung it on the nail that held it in place below the untouched bait. To spruce things up, I squirted a tiny bit of urine below the set in hopes that another marten that passed by would smell the scent of two different animals. If he found it irresistible, there would be another catch in the trap tomorrow morning.

I picked up the marten and admired his thick, beautiful bi-colored fur, a beautiful combination of reddish brown to almost black, and then placed him in the oversized backpack I had strapped to the storage rack on the back of my machine. With that snuggly in place, I headed down the trail to the next set. In the woods it was windy, but somewhat calmer than out in the open. This made traveling much easier. The fourth set held a marten; it was a smaller animal, and a female. I was in awe of her beauty. I quickly made the set again and gave it a shot of urine. While walking back to the machine I noticed a couple of spruce that would work nicely for firewood. After securing my catch in the back pack, I grabbed the saw and bucked the trees into eight-foot pieces. The wood was dry which made it easy to carry in these lengths. These nicely dried trees would make exceptional firewood. After all of this wood was in the sled, I determined that this was the maximum that I could safely carry. This part of my day was done; now it was all about the traps.

I proceeded down my well-marked trail, and by the time I arrived at the last marten set, I had six incredible catches in my pack. This set made it number seven. Another huge male was caught firmly in the trap. I released him, reset the trap, and packed him in with the others. I climbed back on my heavily laden machine and gingerly proceeded down the hill to the area where my two wolf sets were made. Through the trees, I saw movement, a lot of movement. As I closed the distance I saw a small pack of wolves scurry from their feeding spot on the dead bear, which they had now completely dug up. Because I did not know what to expect, I stopped my machine and shouldered my rifle to take a shot if need be. That is when I saw one wolf run up the trail at an angle toward me and bound straight into the second snare that was about thirty feet from the bear carcass. I could not believe what just happened. It was an incredible sight.

A wild, noisy, and confusing struggle ensued. The other three wolves in the small pack stopped running away and stood silently at varied distances from the snared wolf that was still struggling against the snare. Eventually, the securely caught wolf stopped its struggle; it was dead. When all was quiet except for the hum of my still running snow machine, life seemed to go forward in slow motion. It seemed like an eternity that I sat and watched the remaining wolves, their eyes intently locked on the dead wolf. My eyes were locked on them to see what their next move would be. My rifle rested across my lap as a safety precaution. I was not interested in a wolf massacre; however, the bear attack earlier in the year taught me to be aware and ready at all times. Not one wolf moved so much as a hair until I stood up and swung my leg over the snow machine. This was all new to me but I felt like I had to do something to break the stalemate. So, with what seemed like a rational thing to do, I began walking toward the wolves. That is when all mayhem broke loose again.

My initial movement made the wolves scatter, and before I knew what was happening, the snow beneath my feet gave way and I stumbled hard to my right. In doing so, the butt of my rifle slammed the throttle all the way down. My snow machine took off with a roar. It raced down the steep hillside. There was nothing I could do to stop it.
"No!" I screamed into the wind! "No!"

I watched in fearful awe at the sight of the fully loaded sled attached to the snow machine picking up speed and thundering down the hill. In a flash I was back on my feet, but any attempt to catch up with it would be futile.

After a few seconds of total chaos, that seemed more like forever, my whole rig lay on its side at the bottom of the hill. I sprinted down after it, my heart pounding out of my chest. At the bottom of the hill I stood and gazed sadly at my overturned snow machine and sled. I quickly glanced around for any wolves that might have stayed around to watch the show, and then struggled to upright the machine. After a few seconds of wrestling with it, I had the machine back on its track and skis. It did not matter that the sled was still on its side, as the hitch could rotate 360 degrees. I started the snow machine to make sure it still ran. It did. I shut it off and looked nervously around, still no wolves. This was a good thing as I did not need any more to worry about than what was in front of me. I searched intently for damage on my machine and on the sled. There was nothing major that I could see, just a couple scratches and cracks in the hood. The trailer did not fare as well. The hitch bar was bent significantly, and the sled had a long crack on one side where it appeared the load of wood, which was still bound to the sled, had hit with full force as the sled tipped over. The wreckage was a disappointing sight. I glanced back up the hill and thought how amazing it was that my rig did not hit a tree.

"Oh well," I said to myself, "once again, I lucked out." There was nothing more I could say or do.

I took a few minutes to calm down and then turned my attention to my pack that held the fur; everything looked good. I leaned my 30-06 against the seat and walked up the hill to the snared wolf. It was a big female. I figured she was the Alpha female. I expected the others were her pups from this year and previous years. With her gone, they would likely face a certain death during the winter months due to predation or starvation. I made the decision right there that I would set snares for the remainder of the wolves in this pack. This was not a mean-spirited decision, rather, I thought, it was one of mercy. With my snares, I offered a quick death, and as in all natural occurrences, something always benefits from the death of another. This is how I hoped to go when my time came. I wanted to die in the wild and become food for the plants and animals that I shared this land with.

I released the snare's grip from the wolf and dragged her down the hill to my sled. There, I grabbed the needed equipment to set the other snares on the new trails leading to the grave site. As I worked I realized that in spite of all the dangers in the wild land, I was in the right place for me. That I knew for sure. Everything here made sense to me, unlike in my old life where I was confused about all the things that I had lived and seen. There was no confusion here. Everything was black and white.

After all my work was completed, I gathered my equipment and headed downhill and into the clearing at the river's edge. It was then that I noticed there was no wind and no snow falling. In fact, the sun took occasional peaks from behind the clouds. I loosened the straps from the sled and let the wood fall to the ground where it would. I turned the sled upright and checked out the tongue and hitch. They were bent but would work well enough to get me back to camp. I reloaded the wood and strapped it tightly in place. The top two logs produced a ditch between them; that is where I laid the one-hundred-pound wolf. After examining her many-colored fur as it glimmered in the bright sunshine, and being extremely satisfied with my catch, I gave everything a once over. Satisfied that all the wood would stay in place, I started the machine and headed slowly for home.

The cabin looked incredibly inviting as I pulled close to the front door. I went straight inside and stoked the stove and checked the clock. It was two-thirty in the afternoon. It would be dark soon. Back outside, I covered the snow machine with its factory fit cover, carried the wolf to a pile of snow just outside the cabin door, and then grabbed the pack with the seven marten in it and disappeared into the cabin. They would have to be skinned, fleshed, and stretched that night.

Before I started my work, I opened a can of baked beans and a can of corn and put them on the wood stove to heat. I had some ground moose meat outside; it was frozen so I threw the whole pound or so in with the beans and corn. It would make a great meal. To this I added garlic powder, onion powder, salt, and black pepper and then let the concoction to work its magic on the stovetop.

Even though I was exhausted and did not feel like doing any work, I turned my attention to my skinning knives. They were sharp and ready to go. Outside, I found a dozen marten stretchers and a wolf stretcher and brought them in the house and leaned them against the table. Back outside with my best skinning knife I began to skin the wolf. It was immediately apparent that my skinning talents needed work, but with a determined persistence, I prevailed and completed the task with minimal damage to the hide. The tail came out looking great, but around the eyes I got carried away and opened them up too much. It was not a complete disaster, but promised myself that I would do much better on the next one. With that, I went in the house and before skinning the marten, removed my pan of food from the heat of the stove.

I remembered reading that marten are skinned in the same manner as a wolf, case skinned. One big difference between the two is that the marten has a very delicate hide. Because I was learning as I went along, the process of skinning the animals took longer than I had planned. It was seven in the evening by the time I finished everything but the stretching. I went outside to clean up, and then back inside to lather up my hands so that I had all animal residue off of them. I had completely forgot about supper to this point. I was ravenously hungry as I sat down to eat my meal. I did not reheat it, and fell asleep at the table soon after my belly was full. It was ten in the morning when I woke up. The fire was out and the cabin was cold.

Chapter 28
Pelts, Pelts, Pelts

At ten in the morning there was only a pale, dusky light outside. The days were getting really short. That gave me a strange feeling for most of that first winter, but I really did not mind it. There was so much to do, and my daily activities left me little time to contemplate matters that I could not change. In reality, the lack of light had very little effect on me.

After the short consideration of the daylight issue passed through my mind, I became immediately aware that the daylight time was fast dwindling, and that the traps needed to be checked. Only then did I notice the wolf hide and the marten hides piled by the cabin door. When I picked them up, they were cool to the touch. That was a good thing. I was worried they would have dried out overnight. Perhaps it was a good thing that the fire went out and the cabin cooled significantly during the night. I decided to put off checking traps for the day by rationalizing all of my catches would be dead in the traps. I had to get these hides taken care of. All of my marten stretchers were wood, so I pulled the hides on, fur side in, and checked my fleshing job while they were on the stretcher. All fat had to be removed so that the hide dried correctly. I then inserted a tail-cutting guide in the tail where the tailbone used to be and with my knife slit the underside of the tail all the way to the tip. I then turned the pelts fur side out and stretched them to the maximum length without overdoing it. After that was done, I tacked the bottoms in place and slipped spacer rods between the wood and the skin so it would not stick too badly to the wood stretcher. After all, when the hides were completely dried, they would have to come off the stretchers and be stored until it was time to sell them. This was a lot of work, and by the time I was done it was completely dark outside.

I looked around the cabin and admired the drying hides. Beaver, an otter, a bunch of marten, and a wolf, which I still needed to finish. I worked the wolf hide in the same manner as I did the marten. It had a thick and beautiful fur with a shiny black on the back that gradually turned grey as it went down the sides of the hide, eventually turning completely white at the belly. With the spacer rods in place, I leaned the hide against the wall across the room from the stove. I remembered Bill had told me not to allow the fur to get too hot because it could damage the hide by drying too fast. I took a moment to admire my work. It was a satisfying sight, but there was still more to do.

By the time everything was cleaned up, I was extremely hungry, but did not feel like cooking anything. I rummaged around the bins under my bed and found my old standby food, Spam. I popped the lid and shook the preformed meat onto a paper plate and sat there cutting off bite size chunks and chomping them down with nothing else. As I was chewing away, I gave one final thought to me not running the trap line that day. I felt remorse. Skipping a day of checking traps was not something a conscientious trapper should do. I glanced at the clock; it was six pm. I went to the door and opened it to check the weather. There was a light snow falling, but no wind. The thought came to my mind that I needed to go out, but yesterday's accident dominated my memory, and therefore I thought it best to wait until morning. I set the alarm clock for seven am. That would give me plenty of time for breakfast and other chores in the cabin before I left for the day. That morning time would include moving the hides around so both sides dried evenly. I could have the sled loaded and the snow machine gassed up by the time it was light enough to travel safely, and then I would head out.

I finished my evening by reorganizing the supplies under my bunk in order to make room for all the items Bill and Alvin would bring out after Christmas. I glanced at the calendar and guessed it to be December 7th. I was not sure, however. I had little interest in what day it was.

The next morning, I awoke before the alarm clock. Several times during the night I had woke up with excitement pulsing through my veins for the following day's trap line activities. As I lay awake I made mental notes about things to pack in the sled. For sure, I needed some beaver traps and some fox and lynx traps. After I finally rolled out of bed and walked outside to relieve the pressure on my bladder, I made notice of the weather. It was crisp and still, and I anticipated, would be a great day on the trap line.

Since I was up early, I took my time eating breakfast and doing little projects around the cabin. As light began to brighten the winter morning sky, I worked my way outside to prep things for the day.

The snow machine started on the first pull; I was so happy that there was no serious damage to the machine. If there were significant damage, I would have been in one heck of a predicament. I gave one final check of the sled and my equipment and was off down the trail. It was a beautiful day. There was a bit of fresh snow and no wind. After the morning dusk changed to light a blue winter sky appeared and looked as if it had no end.

At the first set I had a nice big marten waiting for me. The second set held another fine specimen. By the time I was to the last marten trap, I had picked up five catches. I made a change of plans. After I checked the wolf snares, I planned to backtrack on this trail and pull all the sets for marten, and then head upstream and set a new line in a fresh grove of spruce that was sure to hold a lot of fur. I rested for a few minutes before jumping on my machine and heading off toward the wolf snares. As I slowly approached the sets, I could see two lumps covered lightly with snow, making it clear to me that I had caught two wolves. I drove past the snares and parked the snow machine down on the frozen river, and then walked the short distance uphill to the sets. Just as I had suspected each trap held a young wolf. I was pleased. I remade the sets with fresh snares, loaded the wolves in the sled and headed back up the trail to pull the marten traps. By the time I was finished, it was about one o'clock. I did not bring a lunch so there was no need to take a lunch break. I headed straight to where I would set my next line.

The first thing I noticed when I entered the spruce grove was that there was an incredible amount of marten sign. Unlike the first place I had set, there was lynx sign as well. I thought this was unusual and wondered if they were enemies, or if the lynx were just passing through. The majority of this grove of trees was closer to the river. There, I noticed more ptarmigan and hare sign. Their presence would draw the lynx to the area. This explained their presence. As an added bonus there was an old entrance to a beaver lodge or beaver feeding chamber in the nearby riverbank. I could see it perfectly well and realized that it at one time had been perfect for beaver when the water was high because they could get in there without becoming prey to the wolves or lynx. Now that the water was low, the hole was exposed and it created a great place to make a natural cubby set for lynx.

I drove up close to the entrance, and then stopped the machine and unpacked a 330-Conibear, some wire, and the pail that held the trap setting material I needed. First off, I threw a hunk of beaver tail in the den hole and then commenced to set the 330-Conibear that would guard the hole and catch anything that tried to get in after the bait. I wired the trap springs tightly to a fallen log just over the hole's entrance. Then I grabbed some sticks and dried river grass to conceal the trap and close off the small areas outside the trap's jaws, the area that a wise lynx might try to pass through if he became suspicious. To finalize the set, I placed a couple of stabilizing sticks to hold the trap from falling over. After that, a squirt of some lynx urine on a clump of branches and river debris that lay on the ground about ten feet from the hole, completed the set. As I looked my work over, I thought this to be the perfect set to capture one of these elusive cats. It was an easy set to check and maintain, and best of all it could stay in place all season, hopefully catching several lynx, and maybe a fox or two.

I took a quick look around for other possible sets to make, and seeing none, mounted my machine and headed uphill into the spruce trees. Mimicking the trap setting process used on the first marten line, I began to make sets at spots that appeared to be heavy with activity. My movements were much more fluid; my previous practice showed the rewards of my hard work. I was making quality sets at a much faster pace, and in no time had twenty sets out for marten. I was impressed with the amount of work I completed during these short daylight hours.

It was pitch black by the time I rolled up to the cabin. The next day I would check the wolf snares first and run the old trail backward, picking up a load of firewood as I traversed through the line. Since I had no plans to set more traps after gathering a sled full of firewood, I would unhook the sled at the cabin and check the new line with the snow machine only. The lynx and marten, if I caught any, would fit in my oversized backpack. Hopefully, these plans would allow me time to check traps, scout some new territory, and get another load of wood.

The winter seemed to be going by incredibly fast. I occasionally found myself missing Bill and Alvin. In reality, it could be as much as a month before I saw them again. I was not lonely; heck, there was no time to be lonely, yet we enjoyed each other's company so much, a guy couldn't but help wanting to see his friends. All of the skinning and stretching of hides took up all of my extra time and prevented me from spending too much time lamenting about their arrival. They would be here soon, and we would fully enjoy that time when it came.

In many ways, I was used to being alone. Back in the days of my old life, I only had a few friends. My parents were in the house every night in the physical sense, but as a family, as weird as it sounds, we operated on an individual basis. So, as I said, this was nothing new to me. Even though I was alone, I was not lonely. I loved my time out here, and knew now that I was never meant to be part of that hustle and bustle world that I escaped from. My peace was the quiet. And, as this fruitful day darkened into this quiet night, I slept soundly because I was tired.

Again, my excitement outpaced the alarm clock. My subconscious mind was well aware of what had to be done on this day. I was happy with my decision to wait until morning to put my logging tools and the chain saw into the sled because the night before there had been just too much work to get done. The number of hides I had drying was remarkable and growing fast. *Tonight*, I thought, *I have to get the beaver off the hoops. That will help to reclaim some space because I can store the dried hides in the rafters overhead where they are up and out of the way.*

The sled was ready and the chainsaw filled with gas and secured in place before I realized I would need lunch. This would likely be a long day on the trail. I had some leftover stew in a pot, and there was enough for a full meal. I strapped that and its lid to the carrying rack on my machine with the idea that I would warm it up over an open fire when I was hungry. I took one final look around for anything I might need, and was off. I had high hopes for the wolf set, but when I got there, all of the snares were still set. It did not appear that any animal had come near the area. I looked things over from the bottom of the hill and could clearly see that all sets were untouched. My thought was that if the lone surviving wolf could not catch food, he would eventually come back for some bear meat. As I observed the site, I felt a little better about the mother bear's death. There were all kinds of birds visiting this spot, pecking at what remained of the meat. It also appeared that many small animals like squirrels and mice made visits to gnaw on the bones. The best thing about the entire bear situation was that nothing went to waste, nature was consuming her. All of the wildlife, plants and animals alike, benefited by her death. It was time to move on.

I jumped back on my idling machine and proceeded up the hill to a spot where I had noticed there were several large trees that would give me a week's supply of wood. The saw fired up relatively easily, even though it was quite cold out. After it warmed up sufficiently, the saw purred along like a happy cat lying in warm sunshine. In what seemed like only minutes, I had a heaping load of firewood strapped securely on the sled. In reality, my work took a couple of hours. It was getting close to the end of daylight, so to save time, I cut across some new territory on my way back to the cabin. At first this seemed like a good idea, but the ground beneath the snow was rough and uneven, making travel slow. I took my time so that I would not experience my second accident involving my snow machine and a load of firewood. After all, I had promised Bill and Alvin, as well as myself, that I would not have any repeat performances. All said and done, I made it safely back to the cabin, where I unhitched the sled and proceeded to the lynx set.

"Bingo!" I shouted. "There is definitely something different about the way that set looks."
As I closed the distance my thoughts were confirmed. There was a dead lynx in my set. Once again, the 330-Conibear did its job effectively. It appeared that the cat flipped over backwards when he first felt the springs constrict on its body, and then lay motionless. There was no sign of struggle. This trap is so fast and so powerful that animals of this size stand no chance against it. This is such a good thing, as I never wanted animals to suffer unduly at my hands.

I picked up the cat still in the trap and admired his size and his mottled fur. I gently laid him back on the snow and returned to my sled for the trap setting tongs and my pail of trapping essentials. I released the big tomcat and made the set again. Rather than put urine back down, I decided to use a gland lure to call in another lynx. Being a territorial animal, the smell of at least three different cat scents in one place, would likely bring in another lynx. I figured it possible that a fox would investigate this set too.

I spent a few minutes running my bare fingers through the thick, smooth fur of the lynx and then put him in my pack and secured the pack in place on the snow machine. I climbed on my machine and made tracks to the first marten set. A nice male was dangling there as dead as a doornail. All in all, that was a great day. I caught five more marten after the first one, and of course, caught my first lynx. The next month proceeded in much the same way. I spent days scouting and collecting firewood; I spent days setting traps and checking traps. To say the least, I was a busy guy. My cabin was full of fur, most of it dried and ready for sale. I hoped Bill and Alvin would return soon. There were several items I needed, especially gas for my snow machine. Mostly, though, I wanted to see my dear friends.

Chapter 29
My Friends Return

      In the middle of the morning, the next day, I was down on the river chopping a hole in the ice with the idea of jigging for and catching a northern pike for supper. A day of ice fishing had been nagging at me since freeze up. Today, I wanted to make it happen. During a moment of rest and a time of admiring my beautiful surroundings, I heard the buzzing of distant snow machines and as I turned in the direction the sound was coming from, saw them come around the bend in the river. It was Bill and Alvin. Before I recognized them, I could see that they were riding side by side on matching snow machines. Their arrival time was perfect because I had asked them to bring me a gas ice auger and some Beaver Dam tip-ups so I could catch more fish by leaving the tip ups out all day, keeping an eye on them from the cabin. The sleds they pulled were full of things that I desperately needed, especially gasoline.

      As they came to stop and the engines died, I let out a rousing whoop of hellos!

"Hello, hello, hello" I said, my exuberance clearly heard in my voice. "Gentlemen, it is so good to see you!"

"Likewise, young man!"

"How are things going out here?" asked Bill. And then went on without waiting for an answer. "I hope you still have all nine fingers."

"Great, I have a cabin full of fur that needs to be sold, and, yes, at last count, nine fingers. Ha-ha, that is funny, Bill."

"I thought so," said Bill. "It took me the whole trip out to get that line to sound good."

"We figured you might have done very well on the trap line. We did too," Alvin piped in.

Alvin kept talking as he took off his parka and shook the snow dust off the back of it.

"Trying for some fish, are you?"

"Yes, I am hungry for fish."

"Excellent, we have all of your fishing equipment and brought you a bucket full of frozen herring for bait."

"Thanks, Alvin," I stated, smiling as I searched the sleds with my eyes.

Bill interjected and said, "Let's go to the cabin before some of the food that should not freeze does just that."

I knew that meant that there were apples and oranges and eggs and other such treats on the sled. With those goodies on my mind, I decided the pike could wait.

Up at the cabin we unpacked the sleds and sorted through all the items that they delivered. This was a good day for all of us. In short time we had all of the items put away and had the gas barrels stored against the cabin wall. Right after that, both Alvin and Bill inspected my furs and then helped me bundle them and place them outside rolled in a tarp ready for transportation. When the men headed back to Fairbanks, they would take my furs with them, sell the fur at the market, and return with my money at a later date.

We settled down to a supper of baked beans, something I ran out of quite a while ago, fried ptarmigan, and fried potatoes. Slices of homemade bread baked by Alvin's wife, Alice, graced the table, and were thickly topped with warm butter.

"A meal fit for kings," Alvin voiced between bites.

And Bill replied, "You got that right, partner. This young man knows how to treat company."

"You guys are so worth it. I was not lonely out here, but I sure did miss your smiling faces."

"We missed you, too."

Bill went on to say that, "We would have come sooner, and even stayed a night at your cabin while on the line, but the year was relatively easy, so we motored home every night."

"Did you guys catch a lot of fur?"

"Yes, we did, and it looks like a bumper year as far as prices are concerned."

Alvin added, "We will see a nice income from trapping this year!"

"Excellent," I said.

"By the looks of my hides, do you guys think I will make some good money?"

"Yes", Bill said, "you will do fine. Your pelts are impressive. You did a fine job of preparation."

"Great, because as you guys know, I do not want to use my inheritance money for myself. That money might as well not be there as far as I am concerned."

"But you should keep it; you never know if you will come on hard times. Unexpected things happen and often times a person needs money to get things back on track," Bill said.

"Yes, I understand that concept, but I am changing out here. I am much different from who I was seven months ago."

"You are, that is for sure, but having that money stored away will come in handy someday, probably sooner than you think."

"Well, then, that makes sense," I said, "but there is one thing I want to spend money on right now."

"What is that?" Alvin asked.

"I want to buy this property. Will you sell it to me, Alvin?"

"Yes, but only the cabin and the five acres it sits on. The rest of the surrounding area is state, federal, or privately-owned land."

"Okay, will you sell me the cabin and the land that goes with it?"

"Yes, I will do that; I figured you might be thinking along those lines, so my family and I discussed this and they all think I should sell."

"Sweet."

"Did you settle on a price?" I inquired, with just a bit too much zest.

"Yes, we did."

"And?"

"Well, this is five acres and it is on the river, so I think a fair price is 85,000 dollars."

"I will take it!"

"No argument on the price?" Alvin asked.

"No. I want this place. No argument on the price."

"Okay, it sounds like we have a deal. To finalize the sale, you will have to come back to Fairbanks in the spring. I will have all the papers drawn up and ready for you to sign."

"That works for me."

"And," Alvin went on to say, "I expect you will be paying cash, so the process will be short and sweet."

"Cash it is. Thanks, Alvin."

Bill finished the conversation by telling me, "We will come to get you with the boat after ice-out, so when the river clears, look for us."

"I will, and thank you!"

Supper was over. It must have been the longest and most enjoyable supper I had ever had. I got up and cleared the dishes and washed the plates, pots, and pans while Alvin and Bill were in and out of the cabin bringing in gear and sleeping bags. I had asked Bill to buy two new cots for them to sleep on. When I finished the dishes, I set up the cots; they were very nice, and when not in use, would fold up and hide away very well. My friends would surely enjoy a restful night of sleep.

Because of how busy we had been, I had not taken full account of my surroundings. As I looked around, my attention was piqued by two tightly bound packages sitting in the middle of the cabin floor, far enough from where I set up the cots, to go unnoticed. Each one about the size of a big suitcase. I didn't know how I hadn't noticed them sitting there until now. In one, I figured, was the tanned bear hide and in the other, the tanned moose hide. I readily cut the heavy twines that secured them and removed the protective canvas wrapper. They were heavy; they were beautiful. I examined each one for its quality, and, ultimately, was extremely happy to have them in my cabin. I placed one on Bill's cot and one on Alvin's cot. They fit perfectly and would add comfort to the sleeping arrangements I had made for my friends.

Bill and Alvin entered the cabin with the last load of gear. They smiled at the sight of their cots set up with the hides on them.

"One good night's sleep coming up," Bill said.

Alvin readily concurred.

"Sleep is what I need!" Alvin said with exhaustion in his voice and a long day of tiredness in his eyes.

We all readied ourselves for the night by finishing last minute preparations around the cabin. I stoked up the fire and lowered the lamplight so that the warm light hugged my friends as they each found their spot in the newly made beds. We talked lightly, but for a long time that night. It was good, peaceful; the way it should be out here in the depths of nature. I do not remember our complete conversation, but do recall drifting off to sleep feeling happy and content to have my friends in my cabin home.

My eyes opened to the bright light of the lanterns and my senses awakened to the smell of bacon and eggs. The aroma of boiling coffee permeated the air. The warm comfort of my bed kept me from leaping up and into the early morning, so I rolled to one shoulder and watched Bill and Alvin work quietly around the stove as they prepared breakfast. Eventually, I yawned and stretched myself out of bed, and with a quick good morning I tumbled out the door to perform my morning duties.

I knew the guys had to get back to town because there were furs to be sold, both theirs and mine. As for me, my trapping season was over unless some fantastic beaver, otter, or muskrat opportunity came up. As a result, I was content to spend the rest of the winter and spring scouting as far out as I could in preparation for future years on the trap line. After I was finished outside, I went back in the cabin to find Bill loading three plates with massive amounts of food. I took my place at the table and thanked them for breakfast.

"Where did you guys learn to cook like this?"

"I was a cook in the army," said Bill. "Alvin was born a good cook."

"Yes, I remember his smoked goose, that stuff was incredible."

"Thanks, Codi. Smoked goose is one of my favorite foods. My dad made it as far back as I can remember. I learned everything I know from him."

"Well, feel free to drop some off here any time," I said slyly. Then, like a clock clicking by a second of time, I changed the subject and asked, "Do you guys think I should peek in on my bear, Pretty Girl?"

"No, I would not," Alvin, said quickly. "If there is something wrong with her, there will be nothing you can do to help her. She is at the mercy of Mother Nature at this point in her life."

To that, Bill added, "If she went in the den fat and healthy, she will be fine."

Okay, I said, "It is just that she has been on my mind lately. I really want her to live."

"She will," Bill assured me. Then, "How is your breakfast, Codi?"

"Awesome!"

"Did you notice how much warmer it is this morning compared to last night?" asked Bill.

"Yes, I did, it is very warm for January."

"We do get these thaws more often these days, and they seem to come earlier in the year," Bill said, sounding a bit dejected over the fact.

"That is for sure. The environment is changing," Alvin said, "and it sure makes snow machine travel more dangerous than it needs to be because of the overflow it creates on the river."

"Codi, you need to be very careful on the ice at all times, but especially during warm ups like this," Bill sternly warned.

"Thanks, guys, I will be careful, and you two, my friends, be careful also."

After a bit more talk over breakfast, and some cabin clean up, we went outside to tighten up the sleds. The men were ready to head home. I did not want them to go, but they had many responsibilities that needed to be taken care of. As the men drove their machines down to the river, I followed with my sled full of ice fishing equipment. I planned on setting up my new tip ups and was hopeful that I would catch a few pike.

We said our final goodbyes on the ice. I cannot explain why, but I had a hard time saying goodbye this time, and a few tears streamed down my face and got lost in the snow as I watched Bill and Alvin motor down the river. My eyes trailed after them until they rounded the first bend. And, sadly, just like that, they were gone. The tears dried up quickly because I knew it was a "so long, guys," not a goodbye.

I turned my attention to fishing, a long overdue excursion, and after some trial and error, managed to drill three holes and set up three rigs baited with herring. While waiting for a fish to take the bait, I spent some time walking around the ice close to shore. It was warm and the ice around the river's edge had water seeping up and pooling in some areas. I did not give it much thought as my mind was almost always focused on animals. I wanted to know where they lived and where they traveled. There was some animal sign, but it seemed as if the cat and fox tracks were not as plentiful as they were earlier in the year.

When I turned back down stream, I saw that one of my tip ups had been sprung and the flag was standing straight up waving in the breeze. I took off at a full run and as I got closer could see the top furiously spinning; that meant there was a fish on the line. I remembered reading about fishing pike using this method. The article stated that the fisherman should let the pike take a second run. The problem was that I did not know how long the flag was up. It had been at least ten minutes since I had glanced at the tip ups. As I knelt down preparing to set the hook, I heard another flag go up. It was a light swish sound that reverberated ever so slightly in the winter wind. I found it pleasing that I could hear a faint sound when there was no other noise to interfere with it.

I watched the second tip up for a few seconds and saw that the fish had stopped its initial run. A few seconds later it started taking line again. I was certain that the second fish was going to swallow the bait so I turned my attention back to the tip up next to me. I gently picked up the tip up and laid it on the ice. At the same time, I laid the line softly between my thumb and index finger without taking up any slack. I did not want the fish to know I was there. I then clamped down tightly on the line, and in one quick motion set the hook. The fish was on. It immediately took line out at an incredible speed, and in doing so, put down a nice burn line on my fingers and in the palm of one hand. I tightened my grip and stopped the run and then began pulling the fish in with the hand over hand method for retrieving the line. I could feel that the fish was heavy, and at one point saw him swim right under the hole. When he came close like that again, I was ready and tried to force him up the hole. It did not work. He was too fast and too strong. Instead, he ran back to the depths of the river, leaving me with a second layer of lines burned on my fingers and hands.

"Damn, that hurts!" I said out loud, but to myself, almost as if Bill and Alvin were standing behind me watching the show. And, then thought, *this fish has a lot more power than I anticipated.* My chance to land the fish would come again. When I pulled him back to just beneath the ice and could tell he was close to the hole, I gently nudged his nose into the hole and then pulled hard. It worked. The huge pike flew out of the hole, throwing water in all directions. Then, a second later, on the ice was a flopping monster of a northern pike. I had no clue how much it weighed, but it was much bigger than the biggest one I caught before freeze up.

After gawking at the large fish for a moment, I came back to my senses and hurled my body toward the next tip up. It was not spinning at all. I quietly picked up the Beaver Dam and grabbed the line and gently began to retrieve it. This time I was better prepared for the fish to run and to prevent myself from getting more line burns. It seemed like I pulled line in forever until I finally felt the slightest change in the line tension; I could tell that something was on the other end. I tightened my grip on the line and set the hook.

"Another big one!" I said to myself, as I put into motion the hand over hand retrieval method. The fish fought hard, but the lessons learned only moments before served me well. I fought the fish for several minutes. There was a lot of give and take, but finally he showed signs of fatigue. At just the right time, I forced the fish's big head into the hole and hoisted his huge body onto the ice. The pike appeared to be identical in size to the first one. I looked in amazement at the two huge fish on the ice and decided not to catch any more until after these were eaten. I tossed the fish in my sled and reeled up all three lines, and with the other equipment gathered up and, in the sled, I headed back to the cabin to clean my fish.

Cleaning the fish came easy to me. All that skinning and fleshing of fur animals improved my knife skills significantly. I could not wait to fry a big mess of fillets. I cut the boneless fillets into pieces about four inches by four inches. Then I got out my best fry pan, a cast-iron beauty, and poured into it about two inches of cooking oil to which I added a thick chunk of butter. The butter would help the flour coating on the fish to brown better. Next, in an old pie tin, I mixed flour, garlic powder, onion powder, salt, pepper, and paprika. In another pie tin I cracked three eggs and poured in a bit of water and mixed it well. On the stove, the cooking oil in the pan was hot and it spattered when I flicked a drop of water into it. I rolled the fish chunks in the egg mixture and then dragged them through the flour mixture, and gently laid them in the fry pan.

The delicious smell of fried fish permeated the entire cabin. I filled the pan so that every square inch of the bottom was covered. As the fish fried, I grabbed a can of beans, and with a few quick turns on the can opener, I had baked beans to go with the fish. After about three minutes, I flipped the fish and after a couple minutes more, loaded the fried fish onto my plate. At the table I ate beans out of the can, and hot fish off the plate. The food was without compare. I wished Bill and Alvin were here to share this meal with me.

Chapter 30
Bad News

The rest of January flew by, as did February and March. I spent a great deal of time out and about exploring, each day going a little further than the day before. On one of these trips, while eating my lunch and enjoying the wonderful spring weather, I came to the realization that I had been on my own for almost a year. The time had absolutely flown by. As I chewed my sandwich and reflected on my past, I pieced together all that had happened. For the first time in a long time, I thought about my parents, and became a little sad that they were no longer in my life. Even though we never had a solid relationship, they still were my mom and dad, and I knew they had loved me. In retrospect, it seemed that I had been an add-on to their lives, never really being part of what they did. Because of that, the dissatisfaction with their parenting of me came early in my life. All of that was in the past, and as always, I was appreciative of my past.

The day of my parents' accident, and the time that followed, until I met Bill, seemed to be a blur. And now, it felt like the accident was years ago. On the other hand, it seemed to me that I knew Bill and Alvin my whole life. I laughed out loud when I recalled meeting Bill, and how we devised a plan to sneak me onboard the ship. Hiding in the trailer was a great plan and it worked like a charm. Meeting Bill at that time was exactly what I needed. Both men helped me to clearly define my purpose in this world. I was now, because of them, living my dream.

Because of Bill's and Alvin's teachings, I had learned to trap, hunt, cut wood, and cook. Added to that, I learned a ton of other things on my own due to trial and error. The biggest mistake I made was my tangle with Pretty Girl's momma. My hand was totally healed now, and not having a pinky finger was no longer an obstacle for me. It did bother me considerably; however, that I was responsible for that bear's death. I worried about those two cubs that were orphaned because of my actions. I was to blame for what happened, but it was over now, and had been chalked up to all that it could be, a learning experience.

My knowledge as a trapper was what I was most proud of. I felt like an old pro, but knew very well that this first year was an easy one. The weather never got too terribly bad. There was plenty of snow, but as Bill and Alvin reminded me, not the usual winter as far as temperatures went. Well, all that was good for me. I was able to target all the animals I wanted to trap except for muskrat. Next year, I would expand my trap line into these newly scouted territories so that I could make enough money to live independently out here in my cabin home.

The day was deathly quiet until my thoughts were interrupted by the sound of snow machines coming up the river, something I had not heard in quite some time. I hoped it was Alvin and Bill. It was not. After a couple minutes of watching their approach, two men pulled up near me, turned their machines off, and doffed their helmets. I immediately recognized them as Alvin's nephews, John and Andy, the same two guys who helped me move in to the cabin last summer. They looked dejected and that made my heart sink. We exchanged a fleeting glance, not really making eye contact. I knew the news they would deliver would not be good.

After a pause that seemed to last a lifetime, Andy, the younger of the two men, stated very matter of factly, "Uncle Alvin and Bill are dead." "What?" I said in disbelief and after I caught my breath. "Dead, what do you mean, dead?"

"They got caught in river overflow on the way back from the trap line last week."

"They drowned?" I asked.

"No, they froze to death!" said Andy.

"Everything they had got soaked because the water on top of the ice was three feet deep. There was no hope for lighting a fire," said John, with disbelief in his voice.

"Froze to death," I muttered, "impossible, not Bill and Alvin."

"The rescue team found them after Alvin's wife notified authorities that he had not returned as scheduled. The rescue team was told that both men were out together on their trap line, so the unit had no problem finding them."

"Please tell me that this is some horrible joke they are playing on me, and that they are going to come bouncing up the river on their machines waving a big fat fur check for me."

"No, sorry," said John. "Sadly, this is the truth."

I was speechless at this point. I could not formulate any more words. My mind was reeling with pain, anger, and frustration. How could my friends be dead? They were my entire life. They gave me this life, and now they are gone. I must have stood there for many minutes before Andy shook me gently and asked me to get ready to ride back to Fairbanks for the funerals.

"Our Auntie," John said "will not consider the funeral taking place without you being there."
"There is plenty of time for us to get back yet today, but there are some detours we must make because of bad ice and stretches of open water," said Andy.
"I will gather my things," I said in a weakened voice.

We jumped on our machines and made the short ride back to the cabin where I packed my big pack with all that I would need. Before leaving the cabin, I made sure I had my cash and bankcard with me. Outside, still in a fog, I fueled up my snow machine and then topped off John and Andy's machines so that we all had enough gas for the trip.

It probably was not the best time for me to consider this, but I looked around and wondered if my days out in the wild were over. I hoped that Alvin had prepared all of the paperwork for the land sale, and that his wife was still interested in selling the property to me. I also had to consider if I still wanted the property. After all, both of my mentors, with a snap of the fingers, were dead. A deep sadness came over me. I could not find a reason why the two people who I loved the most and admired beyond belief, could be dead. It just did not make sense to me. Of all the bad people on the face of the earth, why did two loving and caring men have to die in such a harsh way? I knew it would be a long time before I could come to terms with the answer to that question.

The daze that had set up shop in my brain refused to move out. Still, we had to move on. I fired up my machine and readied it for the ride back to Fairbanks. Andy had told me during our conversation that I would stay with Alvin's wife and family; they had a room prepared for me for as long as I wished to stay there. The ride seemed to take forever; there was no enjoyment for me in the scenery that had always brought great joy to me. The details of the trip were blurred by the never-ending tears that filled my eyes and streaked down my face. I recalled leaving the cabin, but could not recall any of the detours that I knew we had made. When I saw the lights of the city, I popped out of my world of despair only to realize that I had to face a family of grieving people. I had no experience with this sort of thing. I was anxious to say the least.

I thought about Bill. I had known him for less than a year. As far as I knew, he had no relatives; he never spoke of anyone but his sister, and she was dead. Although I knew Alvin very well, I did not know many of his relatives, but did know that his family was quite large and close knit.

It was a good thing that Alvin's house was close to the edge of town because there was not a lot of snow on the ground. Going over barren ground would have been hard on the tracks and skis of our snow machines. After we arrived at the house and parked our machines, we walked across the yard and into the house where a great many people were assembled. The kitchen was full of friends and relatives who were eating and laughing. Some were crying. I could see past them into the living room where pretty much the same thing was happening. Alvin's wife saw us enter and stood to give us hugs and welcomes. Her warm and gentle hug burst the damn that held back a second rush of tears. I thought I had exhausted that reservoir on the ride to town. They streamed down my cheeks like winter snow melt bursting down a rocky slope, silently falling onto the shoulder of Alice's sweater. Eventually, she released her loving arms from around me, smiled up at me, and then kissed my cheek. We both felt better.

The closeness of the family was refreshing; this is something I had never experienced before. Even in the wake of my two best friend's deaths, I found something to smile about. While still standing next to Alice, a pretty young lady named, Jennifer, handed me an empty plate. She told me to head up to the stove and counter to dish up, and then sit down wherever there is space, and eat. I was not hungry, but did as she instructed. Just as I began to search for a place to sit, Jennifer motioned to me that she had a place for me at the kitchen table. I sat down and was readily included in a hearty conversation about some of Alvin's exploits. After listening for some time, it became clear that not only was Alvin a loyal husband, father, and friend; he was also quite the prankster.

One funny story told was how he, many years ago, froze the castors and innards of a beaver, and then in the summer, placed them under the seat of Bill's truck. It just so happened that the summer this occurred was one of the hottest years on record. After a short time, the pieces of beaver thawed and began to stink. The stink did not seem to affect Bill at first, but then the rotten parts putrefied and became unbearable to him. Not long afterward, Bill found what was left of the mess tucked sloppily in the under springs of his truck seat, and realized it was Alvin's work. According to the family, the cleanup work was a spectacle to behold. I had not heard this story before, but by the sound of things, the back and forth pranking was an ongoing event. The stories kept being told, and with the conclusion of each, the house guests roared with laughter.

It was clear to see that the two men were good friends and that this type of shenanigans was a big part of their lives. Maybe that is why they were so endearing to me. I felt myself laughing and talking more as time went on, telling the people around the table all the great things Bill and Alvin had taught me. Now, sadly, there would be no more memories to make with my two best friends.

After the story telling died down, a short and pleasant silence filled the kitchen, much like a kitchen's wood stove's heat rests peacefully in the air of the room. After a period of enjoyment by all, I gently asked, "Does Bill have any living relatives?"
Alice, Alvin's wife, replied after a second or two, "No, there was only the one sister and she died last year."
"That is what I thought because he never mentioned anyone else."
"He was a loner except for times with Alvin," said Alice.

"Yes, he seemed to relish the quiet times," I said. And then,

"Has anyone done anything for his funeral arrangements?"

"Well," Alice said, "he wanted to be cremated, and we are asking for donations so we can give him what he wanted for a funeral."

"I will pay for it," I said without hesitation. "He was my friend, and I have the money to do it," I said a bit forcefully, and then more gently, "I would also like to pay for Alvin's final expenses."

"No," said Alice, "I cannot allow you to do that."

"It would be an honor and a way to pay back Alvin for all he has done for me," I said. I could see that the family was considering my offer.

After some thought, Alice told me, "We are not rich, but we always find a way to pay for everything we need."

"I understand and respect that, but please, Alice, allow me to help you. I have a lot of money and it means nothing to me unless it helps the people I love."

"We have never accepted charity in our lives, yet you make a tempting offer, Codi!"

"It would be a complete honor for me to pay."

"Okay, I am getting old and cannot work like I used to," said Alice with a smile on her face, "You can help us, and for that we are grateful."

"Thank you," was my only response. It made me very happy that the family had accepted my offer.

Shortly after our discussion ended and the normal conversations around the room resumed, Alice began to cry softly. I knew her tears were tears of happiness. Clearly, a burden had been lifted off of her. Everyone felt better and the mood lightened again. The laughter and chatter continued into the night, but dwindled each hour as the guests departed one or two at a time until everyone was gone and silence prevailed in the house.

The funerals would be in a few days, so people were busy making their own arrangements in order to be present to say their final goodbyes. I stood in the kitchen by myself for a few minutes wondering where Alice had gone when Jennifer walked in and offered to show me to my room. I was tired and readily accepted her offer. I grabbed my pack and followed her down a long hallway to the last door. She said, "This is your room, and right across the hall is the bathroom. Don't get lost."

She smiled playfully and pointed in the direction of the bathroom. I nodded to show I understood, but did not recognize her teasing until it was too late to amend my timid, voiceless response.

"If you need anything," she said, "Help yourself. That is how we operate around here."

"Okay, thanks," I murmured.

With that, she was off down the hall to her room. Just before entering her doorway, Jennifer looked back and caught me watching her walk away. "Good night," I stuttered in total embarrassment, realizing I had just been caught checking her out.

"Good night, Codi." She smiled and went into her room.

Chapter 31
The Final Goodbye

Early the next morning I was up and, in the shower, well before I heard any other movement in the house. I could not remember the last time I showered in a modern and fully equipped bathroom. For me, over the last year, cleaning up was standing in a blue plastic sixty-gallon tote filled with lukewarm water giving myself a sponge bath in the middle of the cabin floor. Not the most desirable way to shower, but it kept me clean, and that was the purpose. This, however, was something else, something I had completely forgotten about. After an extended time in the shower enjoying the endless supply of hot water, I felt refreshed and ready for the day. After dressing, I headed up to the kitchen, my nose following the rich smell of brewed coffee. The room was empty except for Jennifer. When I saw her gently moving about the kitchen, my heart raced a bit. I knew last night that I liked her. Seeing her this morning intensified my first feelings. It looked like she was making scrambled eggs and toast to go with the coffee I had smelled earlier.

In the middle of one of her turns, she caught a glimpse of me and said with a smile, "Good morning. The coffee is ready."

"Good morning. Thanks, it smells great in here. Scrambled eggs and bacon?"

"Yes, do you approve?"

"Yes."

"Good. The cream is on the table," she said still smiling broadly and playfully. Hopefully the smile on her face was a confirmation that the feelings I had for her were mutual.

I poured the coffee and then topped it off with the thick cream and took a sip.

"Dang! That is excellent, just the way I like my coffee."

"I am happy you like it. I pride myself on knowing good coffee. Do you want some eggs and toast?"

"I sure do, thanks."

As Jennifer dished up a couple of plates, she told me that Aunt Alice was still sleeping. "This is very much unlike her," she went on, "but the last week was rough on her. I want my aunt to sleep as long as she likes."

"That is a great idea. I will be sure to be extra quiet in the house," I said. "You are a kind person. It is easy to see that you dearly love your aunt."

"I do, and thanks," Jennifer said, shyly, and then quickly changed the subject.

"Later today, she and I will finalize the funeral plans. Would you like to go with us?"

"Yes, I will be happy to go along. Also, since your aunt agreed to let me pay for Alvin's funeral, I can take care of all the financial part of that right away. We will have to stop by a bank first, however. "

"Thanks, it will mean a great deal to Aunt Alice that you will be there."

"Like I said last night, it is my pleasure to do whatever I can for your family."

Jennifer placed a plate in front of me and then set one for herself. We fell silent and ate our breakfasts. The eggs, toast, and coffee were excellent. I felt better than I did the day before, but

217

my mind was still reeling with the loss of my friends, so that is where my thoughts were. The shock had subsided just a bit; however, I still grieved with a deep sense of loss for the two people in this world who I genuinely loved. I reassured myself that things would get better with time. In the meantime, however, so much needed to be done for my friends. All of us would take part in laying our loved ones to rest while grieving their loss. These were hard days, but always, there is some sunshine. I hoped mine was close by.

My mind shifted its thinking to the thought that a bright spark existed between Jennifer and me. I never actually had a "real" girlfriend. That made this experience new territory for me. Even though I knew I liked her, it was not the time or place to pursue a relationship, so I decided to let time do its work. Eventually a time would come when we would know. A few minutes after we finished breakfast, Jennifer began washing dishes. I jumped up and helped her. Soon afterward, Aunt Alice emerged from her bedroom; she looked as if she had been crying.

"Good morning," I said.

"Good morning, Codi. Good morning Jennifer."

"Good morning, Auntie Alice."

"I apologize for my tears," she whispered. "The mornings are the most difficult times for me."

"There is no need to apologize," I said, as I stood and gave Alice a big hug. Jennifer smiled and joined us.

"I will always remember," Jennifer reminded her Auntie, "how you and Uncle Alvin enjoyed the early mornings together."

"Yes, we did, sweetie, yes we did. Your uncle loved to see the sun come up. I don't recall him ever missing a sunrise."

Jennifer poured a cup of coffee for her aunt and mixed in cream and sugar. "Here you go Auntie, just the way you like it."

"Thank you, dear."

"Would you like some breakfast, Auntie?"

"Just toast and butter, Honey."

"On the way," Jennifer said as she skipped to the toaster and dropped in two slices.

Aunt Alice turned her attention back to me and said, "Codi, thank you so much for everything you are doing for my family."

"You are very welcome. I am pleased and happy that I am able to help you."

"I remembered, after I woke up this morning and lay in bed thinking, that Alvin had everything prepared for the land and cabin sale. Do you still wish to buy it?"

"Yes, I do! That has been on my mind also."

"Good, good," she replied. "It will be nice to not have to worry about that piece of property. We can finalize things after the funeral if that is okay with you."

"That will be fine," I said. "It should be a simple process since I will pay cash."

The conversation died, as we sat in silence for some time; each of us in his or her own thoughts.

Finally, the quiet was over. "I suppose," said Alice. "We best get things rolling. Give me a few minutes to get ready, and we can get on with the day."

Jennifer and I spent the time waiting for Aunt Alice by cleaning up the kitchen and washing the remaining dishes that were from the night before. Just as we were finishing up, Jennifer asked me to go outside and start her car so it had time to warm up. I did so, and after a handful of minutes more, Alice appeared back in the kitchen and announced that she was ready to leave. The three of us went outside and got into Jennifer's car. After stopping by the bank, we went to the funeral home to finalize the arrangements that had already been put in place. Alice and Jennifer handled everything for both Bill and Alvin, and when it came time to settle up, I paid the funeral director.

Our third stop was at the Native Alaskan Center. Alice had reserved the hall for the gathering after the funeral, but wanted to be sure the menu was ready to go and that all the foods requested had been made. After this was completed we were set to say our final goodbyes to our dear friends and family members. I paid the staff at the Alaskan Native Center and gave the receipt to Alice. Everything seemed so final at that point. There were other things that Alice wanted to do, but because she was tired out we decided to drop her off at home before Jennifer and I ran the rest of the errands on our own.

One thing I had to do was to go out to Bill's place and figure out the details of his home and belongings. I did not know if he owned his house or rented it. We never once talked about that. Thinking back on the subject, I found it odd that neither one of us ever brought it up in conversation. One thing was for sure, I wanted to save important things from his life, but was unsure of how to do it. Jennifer and I talked it over and decided that the best thing to do was go out there to see what we could find out.

When we arrived at Bill's place, I found out from a neighbor that he rented the house from a man in the area. That was good to hear. My hope was that the owner would allow me access to Bill's belongings. He did. The kind-hearted old man simply asked me to go through whatever I wanted to, and when I was done, to let him know because his plan was to bulldoze the old house. I asked him if I could have until a few days following the funeral. He agreed. I was grateful to the house owner because his kindness gave me the needed time to properly care for Bill's belongings. We departed from Bill's old home feeling that everything would work out nicely.

On the drive back to Fairbanks, Jennifer offered to help me complete all of the work at Bill's place. I readily accepted because I really liked her and wanted to be around her as much as possible. Judging by the look in her eyes and the things we talked about, she liked me too. I had never before entertained the thought of having a serious girlfriend, or, now, how having a girlfriend would affect the life I was living, the life that I knew I would always live. Even with the first pangs of love darting through my body, bouncing between my heart and my brain, I knew that it would not change the way I lived. My life was in the wild. I would never live the fast paced, meaningless life in a city. My hope was that Jennifer wanted the same thing. The last year had taught me this lesson. This meant that if we would grow close enough to consider a life together, she would have to hold the same life goals as I held. I kept my fingers crossed.

The funerals came and went without a hitch. The day of the funerals was a happy day. We rejoiced in the beauty of the lives these two men lived. Again, this was a new experience for me. I had been to a few funerals, including those of my parents, but they were nothing like this experience. The difference was that these two men loved life, and to rejoice in that wonder, is what made the day special. Afterward, Alice spread Alvin's ashes in the river at their goose camp and at their fish camp, places he loved to be. With her permission, I put some of Bill's ashes there too. It only seemed fitting that these two men shared space in the Earth as they did on the Earth. I would spread the remainder of Bill's ashes out by my cabin where he would be forever in the wild. He would be happy with my decision.

A couple of weeks flew by and Jennifer and I grew close, very close. My original thought, that we were falling in love, came true. We spent full days together, and never seemed to tire of each other's company. Even though I did not want to leave Jennifer, the time came when I had to get back to the cabin, and it would have to be by boat. There was so much to do out there in preparation for the upcoming year. I was worried about Pretty Girl. She would most definitely be out of her den. I hoped she was safe. The thought of my little bear, which I had temporarily forgot about until now, intensified my need to return to the cabin as soon as possible.

It seemed odd to me, but I knew it was love. I loved Jennifer, and on the night before I headed to my cabin, she told me she loved me and that she wanted to live with me in the life I had created out at my cabin home.

Knowing that she loved me and wanted to live in the wild was extremely pleasing for me to hear and internalize. The thought of leaving her resurfaced and I did not like that, but after a long discussion about our future, we agreed that this was the best plan of action. We agreed that she would take Alvin's boat up to my cabin in two weeks, and from there we would finalize our plans.

Chapter 32
Back to the Cabin

My snow machine would have to stay behind. The snow was completely gone and the river was wide open as the year was warmer than normal. John and Andy agreed to run me upriver, and I was grateful for their offer. Everything was settled for my two friends, Bill and Alvin, and I was happy about that despite the fact that they were no longer with me. I found a couple of keepsakes in Bill's house, and hundreds of traps and a dozen or so tubs that were full of other trapping gear. I rented a storage shed in Fairbanks until I could find time to sort through everything. I had to decide what to do with all of the traps. I wanted to keep some to use on my trap line, and keep some to hang on the cabin wall in memory of Bill.

The ride upstream was uneventful. I bought two big pallets of canned and dried goods, so the boat was loaded heavily. John and Andy had work obligations, so they quickly helped me unload and stack everything on the beach. After saying our goodbyes, they drifted away from shore, started the motor, and disappeared around the bend. I was on my own again. It felt good, yet there was a twang of loneliness in my being. I missed someone.

I looked around quickly for Pretty Girl. I did not see her so I grabbed a couple cases of dried goods and headed up the bank toward the cabin. Right as my eyes crested the bank, I looked up and saw a bear at the front door of the cabin. I was startled, but then in a loud whisper said, "Pretty Girl, is that you?"

She turned and looked at me, stared for a moment, and then slowly walked my way. Even though she seemed a bit cautious, I think that if she had more than a stub for a tail, it would have been wagging wildly behind her.

"You look good, little girl," I said. "Do you remember me?"

She stopped her walk toward me when we were about twenty feet away from each other. I stopped too. She seemed to become keenly aware of her instincts. Pretty Girl turned her nose to the air and sniffed hard as she danced short steps to the left and to the right, eventually returning to the trail. I think, for a moment, she was not sure of who or what I was, but was still happy. It was not a scary moment for either of us, rather more like a formal identification and a formal greeting.

After our little introductory session was over, I took the first steps toward my little bear. She looked pretty good; in fact, she looked very good because I was skeptical that she would make it through the winter. I did not know how she would react to my touch, so I walked right on by her, talking gently to her the entire way back to the cabin. I opened the cabin door, looked around to be sure all was in good shape, and then set down my load on the table. It was good to be home.

Pretty Girl had followed me and now stood in the doorway, half in the cabin and half out of the cabin; she was again sniffing the air heartily, this time, I guessed, out of hunger.

225

"Do you want something to eat, Pretty Girl?" "Sure, you do." I answered for her. I looked around the cabin and considered what was still stacked down on the beach. Under my bed I found cans of green beans and corn. With them, I threw together a tasty mixture of cold veggies and dumped a can of spam and a can of stew on top for good measure. I put the big bowl of goodies on the floor. It only took Pretty Girl a second to realize that this was a good situation. She came in to eat the food and then licked the bowl clean. As a special treat, I poured a cup or so of honey in the bowl. This kept her busy until I finished carrying all my supplies to the cabin.

Needless to say, our bond had lasted through the winter. Pretty Girl and I, I hoped, would be friends for life. Even though I knew we would drift apart to some degree, because that is the natural workings of such a relationship, I figured there would always be that sense of recognition and respect.

After getting resituated in the cabin, I decided that this would be a good time for me to consider an addition to the cabin. To expand my trapping endeavor, and have a life with Jennifer, more room would definitely be needed. An upper level would be nice for sleeping. As I thought more about this, I finalized the idea and started drawing up plans. I had no particular training in the area of construction, but knew I could do it. I made a list of tools and materials that would be needed. As an afterthought, I decided to build a covered wood shed big enough to serve as a carapace for a huge supply of firewood, and big enough to park my snow machine under. I figured all the materials could be delivered on a big barge type boat by its owner, who I would have to hire.

After the planning work was completed, I started to think more and more about Jennifer. I had to find work to do so I could keep her in the back of my mind rather than at the front of my mind in a dreamy state that prevented me from accomplishing work that needed to be done. I cut firewood daily for two weeks and carried it back to the cabin one eight-foot log at a time. It was not too hard to do as most of the trees were standing dead timber, and well dried out. Pretty Girl was by my side on most days. I thought about rigging a harness for her and have her pull the sled up and down the beach. With a little more thinking I realized I had nothing with which to make a harness. Ultimately, I figured, not using Pretty Girl's bear strength would avoid a great disaster. As I pictured the scene in my head, having a panicked bear run frantically away with a log filled sled strapped to her was a real possibility. No, it was best that I keep collecting firewood with the proven method of shouldering it and carrying the wood home and put the bear as a horse theory to rest.

After the chore of collecting wood was completed, I spent most of my time leveling the earth in the spot I planned to build the addition. That job created a day's worth of back-breaking work. It was well worth it, and everything there looked ready for the building process to begin. If all worked out as planned, I would haul some materials up with me when Jennifer escorted me back to the cabin after our trip to Fairbanks. Either that, or, as I recalled my earlier plan, would put it all on a hired rig and have it brought upriver on that commercial vessel.

Finally, after what seemed like an eternity, the day came when Jennifer would arrive. I impatiently paced the river shoreline glancing downstream every second or two, thinking I had heard a motor racing upstream. My active anticipation fooled me several times. Finally, I heard a real engine. The butterflies started dancing in my gut and in my chest.

This must be love, I thought.

Sure enough, there, coming around the bend was Jennifer in that big boat, her long black hair flowing behind her in the wind. As she closed the distance I could see her beautiful smile and her bright teeth shining in the early day sun. She was a beauty to behold.

Jennifer expertly slowed the boat and gently bumped the bow against the shore, and threw the rope to me all in one swift motion.

"You have done this before," I said, beaming proudly at Jennifer.

"Yeah, a time or two. My whole life has been in camps and on the river. I love the life that subsistence living offers."

"Me too." I quietly said, because I never really put a term to it before--*subsistence*--I repeated in my mind. I liked the sound of that.

Jennifer jumped from the boat and wrapped her arms around me and said, "It is so good to see you. I have missed you."

"I have missed you too."

With that she planted a big kiss on my lips.

I wrapped my arms around her and together, with no other words spoken, we hung onto each other and felt our love envelope us. That was a great day.

After a moment or two, we grabbed her things and walked to the cabin. In all my exuberance, I rambled on about all of my plans and showed her the work I had done over the last two weeks. She was impressed.

"Now," Jennifer playfully teased, after the outside tour was over. "Let's see what kind of house keeper you are."

"Okay, here it is," I said, as I swung the door open. Just as we were stepping in, I heard Pretty Girl come around from the backside of the cabin and brush the backside of my legs. She seemed completely oblivious to Jennifer's being with me, but only a second later, got a whiff of her, grunted and woofed, startling herself as well as Jennifer. Each of the two of my loved ones wasted no time running in different directions, Jennifer into the cabin, and Pretty Girl to her den site on the hill. I fell to the ground laughing hysterically for a full minute, and then got up, still laughing, and entered the cabin. Jennifer was not happy with what had happened. She had my 30-06 in her hands, and because it was always loaded, was ready to use it.

Her anger and fear were plain to see. Finally, her glare subsided and she said in an inquiring tone, "After witnessing your reaction to that bear, I get the feeling you and that creature are friends. Am I right?"

"Yes, we are friends. Come on, let's go up the hill and get you two acquainted."

"Friends with a bear? Are you sure?" she asked, still on the edge of the bed, the rifle now lying beside her. "Yes, she will be fine after she gets to know you. She has been with me since last summer. I killed her momma."

"Why?"

"It is a long story that I will tell you on the way back to town; I am not proud of it, but have dedicated my life to this cub in an attempt to make things right."

"That is so sweet of you, to take care of her like this. I wish you would have told me about her sooner. I have not been that frightened in a long time."

"Sorry," I said. "I guess it was quite a shock for both of you."

After a few more minutes, Jennifer had settled down enough to take my hand to walk up to Pretty Girl's den. When we got there, she was curled up inside with her head slightly poking out of the entrance, looking like a sad puppy.

"Pretty Girl, this is Jennifer," I said formally. "Jennifer, this is Pretty girl, now shake hands."

My humor made Jennifer laugh and I think sent good vibes to my little bear. She inched her way out of the den and sniffed Jennifer's hand while making little unthreatening grunts.

"You can touch her. She is kind of like a dog, and really enjoys being scratched."

"Okay," she said, as she reached out to Pretty Girl, "but this is a bit nerve wracking. I never touched a living bear before; hey, this is pretty cool."

"Yes, it is. You two will be old friends before you know it."

After the introductions were successfully completed, the three of us must have looked like a family as we traipsed single file down the hillside to the cabin. Family, a sensation that was relatively new to me, and quite different from my family feeling with Bill and Alvin. Just like my time with them; however, my feeling of lifelong togetherness felt strong with Jennifer.

Because her Aunt Alice was worried for her safety, Jennifer and I were required to return that same day. So after we unloaded supplies that Jennifer had brought with her, and loaded everything that needed to go with us, we said our goodbyes to Pretty Girl at the cabin door and walked to the river bank. Pretty Girl followed us all the way to the river, but did not come down the bank. I trotted back up to her and gave her a big hug. Jen watched and knew that Pretty Girl was very dear to my heart.

"We are family, Jennifer. Me, you, and Pretty Girl. What do you think about that?"

"I like it." Jen said, smiling her approval.

"Well then, I guess there is no better time for me to ask you to be my wife and join me and this cute little bear in our life in the wild."

"Do I get a ring?" She asked in her playful voice.

"As soon as we get back to Fairbanks, any ring you want." I said, smiling broadly.

"How can, a girl refuse that offer."

Jennifer jumped out of the boat and climbed the bank to where Pretty Girl and I waited. She gave both of us a hug and a kiss, and then said, "Yes!"

Chapter 33
Commitment to a Life in the Wild

It was a fun time back in Fairbanks, but was now almost June. While we were away from the cabin, Jennifer and I got married, but did not go on a traditional honeymoon. Neither of us wanted that. Time was flying by and we were feeling the need to get back to our home in the wild. We had to get back early in order to get things set up for the trapping season and for the onset of winter.

Together, Jennifer and I bought and paid for all the materials and tools to build the addition. Included in these were our drawn-out plans for the addition, that I somehow knew in the back of my mind were not finalized. There were stacks of lumber, shingles, and beams. On a pallet next to those items were boxes of screws and boxes of nails. I am sure that we over-bought on several items, but as we looked at the situation, we were planning to live out in the wild for our entire life time. That meant whatever was left over we would find a use for down the road.

We made plans to ride out with the boat master and unload the materials on the beach with his help, and carry them up to the cabin as needed. This would work out perfectly, as we could spread out the heavy lifting and carrying days so as not to wear ourselves out. Our plans were set, and there was a ton of work to do. There was nothing better to do but get going with the trip.

The last night in Fairbanks, we took Aunt Alice out for supper and then spent the entire evening with her at home. It was a great time. She and Jennifer had always been extremely close, so I knew their parting was not easy. We made it clear that Alice was welcome anytime, and since we had no way of contacting each other, we would be looking for her all the time.

The next morning, the three of us rose early and enjoyed a simple breakfast of eggs and toast. We cleaned up the dishes and then Alice gave us a ride to the river where our boat master was waiting for us. He was somewhat of a pushy guy, and before we were out of the car, he reminded us that we were late.

"Sorry," I quipped. "The goodbyes took longer than expected.

"Okay," he said more gently. We have a long day and a lot of work to do, so we best hit the water in a few minutes."

"Thanks," I said. "We will say a quick bye to Auntie and then get on board."

"Sounds good. I will warm up the engine."

I looked over and saw that both Alice and Jennifer were crying. That made me feel bad. In a way, I was separating them, and that hurt me, as I knew it hurt them. I also knew that Aunt Alice would not have it any other way. She had lived, and continued to live her life her way, and would expect nothing less for her niece. We all knew it would take a little time for all of the emotions to settle into place.

I walked over and joined them in a group hug. Aunt Alice gave me that loving yet stern talking to, that reminded me that I must take care of Jennifer and take care of myself. I told her that I would and that we would see her soon. As a final gesture, Alice gave each of us a hug and a kiss. Her last words to us were, "I love you both." We returned the loving words and waved goodbye from the boat as we motored upstream to our cabin home.

Printed in Great Britain
by Amazon

84183616R00140